EARTH SHATTERING

Blue Crystal Time Travel Book 1

Cathy Peper

Gluesticks and Gemstones

St. Peters, MO

Copyright © 2017 by **Cathy Peper**

All rights reserved. No part of this publication may be reproduced, distributed or transmitted in any form or by any means, without prior written permission.

Cathy Peper/Gluesticks and Gemstones
549 Wyatt Drive
St. Peters, MO 63376

Publisher's Note: This is a work of fiction. Names, characters, places, and incidents are a product of the author's imagination. Locales and public names are sometimes used for atmospheric purposes. Any resemblance to actual people, living or dead, or to businesses, companies, events, institutions, or locales is completely coincidental.

Book Layout © 2017 BookDesignTemplates.com

Earth Shattering/Cathy Peper. -- 1st ed.
ISBN 978-1-946548-02-3

To my Children: Kyra, Connor and Courtney

Other books by Cathy Peper:

Regency Romances:

The Seventh Season-Purchasing link: books2read.com/u/mBewMy

Peyton and the Paragon-Purchasing link: books2read.com/u/47kjyR

Contents

Chapter 1 1
Chapter 2 11
Chapter 3 19
Chapter 4 27
Chapter 5 33
Chapter 6 41
Chapter 7 51
Chapter 8 59
Chapter 9 67
Chapter 10 75
Chapter 11 85
Chapter 12 95
Chapter 13 111
Chapter 14 115
Chapter 15 123
Chapter 16 131
Chapter 17 143
Chapter 18 151
Chapter 19 159
Chapter 20 169
Chapter 21 179
Chapter 22 185
Chapter 23 191

Chapter 24 197
Chapter 25 203
Chapter 26 211
Chapter 27 217
Chapter 28 225
Chapter 29 231
Chapter 30 237
Epilogue 241

Chapter 1

As usual, Tori arrived at the music studio where she taught violin lessons half an hour early. She liked to prepare for her students and squeeze in a bit of personal practice time before things got busy. She had just placed the violin under her chin and run the bow over the strings when the studio manager burst in the door, without knocking.

"I need to see you in my office, pronto," he said and stalked off.

In spite of his urgency, or perhaps because of it, Tori carefully placed the violin in its case and took a sip of her diet soda before dragging herself down the hall. She knew it wasn't going to be good news. "What's up, Matt?" she asked.

"Sit." Matt pointed toward the chairs that were usually reserved for parents signing their kids up for lessons. Tori perched on the edge of one of them. Though the seat was padded, she didn't feel comfortable.

"I've received another complaint about you."

Tori squirmed. Jason's parents, she assumed. "About what?"

"You accused Jason of not practicing."

"He doesn't."

"That's not your concern. You can suggest to him or his parents that he practice more often, but you can't call the kid a liar when he claims he did what he was supposed to do."

"I never called him a liar."

"You implied it."

Tori rubbed her thumb against the arm of the chair. "It won't happen again."

Matt slammed his hand down on the desk. "Now who's lying?"

Tori leaned back in her chair. She'd known complaining to Jason's parents about his practice habits was a mistake almost before she said it, but when it came to her music, the ugly beast of perfectionism reared its head. Still, Matt seemed unreasonably angry. "I will try my best to say only good things about my students to their parents."

Matt pushed away from his desk and paced the length of the room. Since his office was the same size as the small cubicles where the teachers gave lessons, this wasn't very far. "Some of your students love you, Tori. Their parents can't say enough good things about you."

Those would be the students who showed promise, or at least made a genuine effort. "I love them as well."

"That's what makes this so difficult." Matt ran a hand over his head, messing up hair that already had a tendency to stick up in strange places. "But I have to let you go. Pack up your things and leave the keys to your room with me."

Her mouth fell open in shock and she gripped the arms of the chair. *This couldn't be happening.* "What about my students?"

"They'll be split up between the other violin teachers."

There were two other teachers at the studio who taught string instruments. Tori shared an apartment with one of them, but neither was as good a musician as she was. "My students won't be happy."

"Maybe not, but they'll adjust. Jason's parents have influence. They might tell their friends not to come to this studio or make nasty posts on our Facebook page. I can't risk keeping you on. It's bad for business."

Tori glanced at her watch. She felt sick to her stomach. "My first student will be here in twenty minutes."

"No, they won't. All your lessons have been canceled for today."

Tori stood, her legs shaking. Tears threatened. *I won't cry! Not in front of Matt.* She dug into her jeans pocket for her keys. With trembling fingers, she dug her fingernail into the coiled rings, former apartment, Tori thought bitterly. Of course, with no job, the commute wouldn't be an issue.

She had already planned to drive down there tomorrow—Anne had helped her get a gig playing weekends in December at one of the historical homes for their Christmas celebration. She would just go down a day early.

"Tori, are you okay?"

Tori looked up. Ned, her neighbor one flight up, stood on the landing gazing at her with concern. Tori took a great gulp of air. She had been so deep in thought she hadn't even heard him approach. "Not really. Stacy threw me out of our apartment and I can't fit all my stuff in my car."

"Why would she do that? You been eating her food out of the fridge?" He laughed, then sobered, perhaps realizing she didn't appreciate his humor. "No, seriously, did you have a fight or were you late with the rent?"

"I've always paid on time, but it seems Stacy wants her boyfriend to move in."

"Oh, man, that's harsh. And right before Christmas, too."

Tori hadn't given the upcoming holidays much thought. She wasn't very religious and didn't celebrate much since her mother's death. "Well, if Santa doesn't give me a storage locker for Christmas, I'll be giving away much of my stuff."

"I've got some extra room. Do you want to put it in my place?"

"Oh, I don't know, Ned." She barely knew the man. They had gone out on a date once, but nothing had come of it. Since then they'd done no more than occasionally hang out at the pool together.

"It's no bother. At least until you find someplace else."

It would be a huge relief to store her things rather than abandon them. "Well, if you're sure. I don't want to be any trouble."

"Let me give you a hand." Ned reached for a random box.

"Wait. I've sorted them into two piles. These are going in my car. If you could take the rest..." She was still hesitant.

"No problem." Ned grabbed a box of nonessentials and Tori began carrying the boxes containing her clothes and music paraphernalia to her car. These were followed by sealed boxes of things from her mother's house. She stuffed her car until it was filled to bursting, but couldn't fit everything. A few of her mementos would have to stay with Ned.

"I really appreciate your help," she said as Ned stacked the last box in his living room. "I'll have them out of here as soon as I can." Maybe she could rent a storage unit in Ste. Genevieve. It was sure to be cheaper there than in St. Louis.

"Don't worry about it." Ned gave her a carefree grin. "Hey, do you have a place to stay?"

"Yes, I'm going to stay with my friend, Anne."

"Anne? Isn't she the one who lives out in the boonies somewhere?"

How does Ned know where Anne lives?

"I met her at one of the complex pool parties."

Tori relaxed. She had invited Anne and her little girl to come to the apartment and swim at the pool. "Ste. Genevieve is a lovely, historic town. I'm not sure Anne would appreciate you referring to it as the boonies."

"Whatever. It's a long haul. Why not stay here?"

"Oh, no," Tori said quickly. "You've done quite enough. I need to go to Ste. Genevieve anyway—I'm working there this weekend."

"It's only Thursday. You're welcome to stay here tonight. You've had a rough day and the weathermen are calling for snow. You could leave tomorrow morning when you're fresh."

Although it wasn't even dinner time, it *had* been a very long day. Tori glanced out the window and saw a lazy snowflake twirling down from above. Why did the weathermen have to be right today of all days? But she just didn't know Ned that well.

"Your choice, no pressure," he said, holding his hands out in a placating gesture.

Why not? She didn't feel up to tackling rural roads in the snow and Anne wasn't expecting her until Friday. "If you're sure, Ned. I don't want to be a burden."

"No problem. We can have dinner at the Chinese place down the street."

Uh-oh. It was starting to sound like a date. "I don't know. If I leave now, I might be able to beat the snow."

"Traffic will be a bear. If you wait until tomorrow the snow plows will have taken care of things. Besides, you gotta eat, right?"

Tori offered a weak smile. She was overreacting. "Right."

"How about I meet you at the restaurant in an hour? I have some errands to run. You can stay here, I guess..."

"No, I have some things to do too."

They stepped out of the apartment and Ned locked the door behind him. "See you in an hour," he said and took off down the stairs. Tori followed more slowly. Was she making the right decision? Should she press on to Ste. Genevieve today? When she reached the ground floor and saw the snow-covered grass, as well as the dusting that was building up on the pavement, she decided she had made the right call. She didn't want to end up in a ditch somewhere.

"Of course." They picked their way across the parking lot, being careful not to slip on the snow which now covered the paved areas as well as the grass. Only a few new flakes fell, however, and Tori could hear the rumbling sound of a snowplow hard at work clearing the streets. When they reached her car, she tossed a few items, that had been sitting in the front seat, including her violin, into the back, which was already full of the boxes that hadn't fit in her tiny trunk. Ned slipped inside, his legs cramped in the space. He tried to move the seat back, but the boxes got in his way. "Sorry," Tori said.

"No matter. It's a short drive."

Grateful for that, Tori cautiously pulled out onto the road. In her current financial situation, the last thing she needed was an accident. The roads had been salted and plowed, though, and weren't too bad. Within minutes, she reached the apartment complex and parked in her usual space. "Let me just grab a few things." Tori searched around until she found the box that appeared to contain her bathroom supplies. She also made sure to bring her violin, since she didn't want to leave it in the car when it was below freezing.

Ned led the way up to his place. She had been too upset earlier to notice his decorating style, but now she saw that although he hadn't done much to brighten the plain white walls and neutral counter tops, it also wasn't as messy as she might have expected a bachelor pad to be. There was clutter—mail piled on an entry table, magazines and papers spread out on the couch, and a jumble of sports equipment trying to escape its basket in the corner—but no stacks of unwashed dishes or bags of empty take-out containers. She dropped the box containing her toiletries on top of the other boxes and set her violin case on the ground beside them.

"Have you lived here long? You were already here when Stacy and I moved in, right?" That had been two years ago, after they graduated college.

"Three or four years, I think."

And he hasn't hung a single picture in all that time? Weird, or maybe it's a guy thing. She shrugged out of her coat and draped it over a kitchen chair.

"Want to watch something on Netflix?" Ned hung his coat on a hook at the back of the door.

"Sure." *That'll be a lot easier than trying to make conversation.*

Ned turned on the TV and tossed her the remote. "You can pick something out."

Tori sat on the couch, which had seen better days, and browsed through the selections. Nothing romantic, she quickly decided. No horror, either. Action-adventure should do the trick. "How about *Die Hard?*"

"That's fine. Want something to drink? I've got a bottle of wine, or there are beers in the fridge."

Tori hesitated. She wasn't much of a drinker, but if any day deserved a drink, this was it. "Wine, please." She heard the pop of a cork releasing and then Ned set two glasses on the coffee table before plopping down beside her. She started the movie and took a sip of wine. Drier than she preferred, but still drinkable.

"Is it good? I usually drink beer, but the man at the liquor store recommended this wine."

He went to the liquor store? Was that one of the errands he ran earlier? Tori felt uneasy again. She took another sip and set her glass down. "I like it." It wasn't a total lie. The second sip had gone down easier than the first and she suspected it was a quality vintage even if she wasn't knowledgeable enough about wine to know the difference.

Ned drained his glass in a thirsty gulp and refilled it. Tori was tempted to "accidentally" push the bottle off the table. "I've always loved this movie," she said instead.

"Yeah, it's all right." Ned placed his arm around her shoulders.

All right? Bruce Willis and Alan Rickman? She wriggled, trying to pull free from his arm, but that only made him draw her in tighter.

Take it easy, just watch the movie. Don't make a big deal about things. She focused on the TV, trying to ignore his touch.

That worked fine for a while, but then he began massaging her shoulders. It felt good—she was still very tense—but she didn't like the way things were going and didn't want to give Ned the wrong impression. She ducked out from under his hand and stood. "I'm going to take a bathroom break."

"It's down the hall, probably in the same place yours was. I think these units are all the same."

"Seem to be," Tori agreed. She found the bathroom with no trouble. As she was washing her hands, she wondered how to deal with Ned.

When she came back to the living room, she found that he had refilled both of their glasses. She sighed. "You know, Ned, I'm really tired. Would it be okay if we skipped the rest of the movie and I made up the couch? I want to get an early start tomorrow."

"I don't care about the movie, I've seen it a dozen times already. But no need to cut our evening short." He twirled his glass by the stem. "Come finish your wine."

"I've had enough, thank you." She sat down, but beyond his reach.

Ned took another gulp, watching her over the top of his glass. "I've always thought you were really pretty."

"That's nice of you to say." Tori clasped her knees.

"No, I mean it. I always thought it was strange that you don't seem to have a lot of boyfriends."

"I don't think who I date is any of your business."

"Maybe not, but I can't help but notice, living in the same building. You know that gal on the first floor? I think she belongs to the man-of-the-month club." He laughed and Tori wondered if she was imagining the hint of malice in it.

"This conversation is getting us no where. This was a big mistake. I think I'll head on down to Ste. Genevieve."

"It's late and it's still snowing."

"The snow had nearly stopped by the time we left dinner."

"Maybe it started back up."

"I'm sure I'll be fine." She stood, but so did he. When he'd been helping her move boxes his rangy strength had come in handy, but now it seemed dangerous.

"You don't need to leave."

"I think I do."

She moved toward the door and he moved with her. "You still owe me for dinner."

Tori narrowed her eyes at him. "I offered to pay."

"And now you will."

"Step out of the way and I'll get my purse."

He closed the distance between them and pressed her up against the wall. "I came to your rescue today, carried your boxes, took you to dinner. You owe me."

Tori's breath caught in her throat. He loomed over her, seeming twice her size. "I never asked you to do any of those things. I thought you were my friend."

"If you thought I was your friend, why didn't you ever have me over?" Ned ran a finger under her chin.

"I work a lot." True enough, though she had never given Ned much of a thought except when she ran into him at the pool or grocery store. She certainly had never considered him a threat. Her mother had forced her to take self-defense lessons, but that had been years ago and she'd never applied the techniques in a real-life situation. She wasn't sure she even remembered them. "All work and no play, that's me," she said, forcing a chuckle.

"And where has that got you? Kicked out on the street. I think you should rearrange your priorities."

Jerk that he was, he had a point. "I'll think about your advice tomorrow. Right now, you need to let me go." She tried to put as much authority into her voice as she could, but even she could hear the shakiness in her words, and he was standing close enough to feel her body trembling.

"Right now, you need to give me a kiss," he said, mimicking her.

She slid to the side, but he followed, lowering his head and pressing his mouth against hers. She fought to get away, but he only increased the pressure, grinding his lips against hers and forcing her head against the wall. "Stop!" she tried to say, but he was robbing her of air. Bile rose in her throat and she thought she might be sick. She slapped at him, but her blows only made him laugh.

"I knew you were a fiery one," he said and slammed her head against the wall.

Pain exploded in the back of her head. Her vision dimmed and she thought she was going to pass out. *This can't be happening.* She'd been fired, evicted, and now she was going to be raped. A tear trickled down her face and dripped onto her sweater. She still felt dizzy and was only vaguely aware of Ned thrusting his tongue in her mouth and smashing her into the wall.

Suddenly her mouth filled with blood and Ned made a strangled cry as he pulled away from her. She'd bitten down on his tongue without even realizing it. Taking advantage of the space, she stomped as hard as she could on his foot and drove her elbow into his stomach. When Ned doubled over, she slipped away from the wall and ran for the door. She paused long enough to grab her violin from the wall of boxes and snatch her coat off the back of the chair before bolting out onto the frigid landing.

"What the hell?" she heard Ned yell behind her, but he didn't seem to be coming after her. Would he really have forced her? No time to worry about that now. She ran down the steps, glad that the roof kept them relatively free of snow. She raced to her car, relieved she had parked it in a familiar spot, pulled the keys from her jeans pocket and pressed the unlock button. She pulled the door open and threw herself inside, nearly catching her foot in her haste to close the door behind her. Only when she heard the sound of the locks engaging did she allow herself to take a deep breath.

She was safe. There was still no evidence of pursuit. The car was locked and she could drive away. She took a second to assess. Other than the back of her head, which felt tender when she ran her hand over it, she was unhurt. She thought a small bump might be forming, but didn't think it was anything serious. She was shaking, from the rush of adrenaline and the cold. She set her violin on the passenger seat and struggled to put on her coat. It wasn't easy in the confines of the car with shaking hands, but she managed. Then she inserted the key, started the car, and drove out of the parking lot.

Where should she go? She was in no condition to make a long drive and didn't want to show up at Anne's house in the middle of the night. She considered returning to the library, but no one would be there now, and a lone car in the parking lot might invite trouble. Instead, she drove to the twenty-four hour Walmart. There was always someone there, day or night. There were only a handful of cars scattered across the huge parking lot, but they projected an air of normalcy. Tori parked in an nearly empty section as far away from the bright security lights as possible. She would sleep here and make the drive in the morning.

She tried to push her seat back, but found, as Ned had earlier—it seemed like days ago—that it wouldn't go more than a few inches. She took what she could get and also reclined the seat as far as she possible. It was cold, but she didn't think it would be safe to leave the engine running. Burrowing into her coat, she closed her eyes.

Chapter 3

Tori awoke to a banging on her window. She looked up, startled, blinking her eyes at the sudden influx of bright light. A cop, a middle aged man with short dark hair, stood next to her car. She turned the key and lowered the window.

"Are you all right in there?" he asked.

"Yes, fine." The night had dragged on, but she must have fallen asleep eventually.

"What are you doing here?" the cop asked, his eyes narrowed in suspicion as he gazed at her over-stuffed back seat.

"Lost my lease. Gonna move in with a friend today."

The cop's hard eyes softened slightly. "You do that. You can't be sleeping in parking lots, you know. It isn't safe."

Safer than the alternative. A hysterical laugh bubbled in the back of her throat, but she forced it down. She didn't think the cop would understand and she had no intention of reporting what had happened with Ned to the authorities. It would be her word against his and she just wanted to put last night behind her. She still thought she might have overreacted, and the police might think the same. Of course, he had slammed her head against the wall.

"Yes, sir. I'll be on my way now."

The cop nodded and strode back to his car. He kept an eye on her as she stepped out of her own vehicle and stretched out the kinks of sleeping in a tight space. She turned to grab her purse, but it wasn't there. Tori closed her eyes as panic washed over her. She remembered running for the door, grabbing her violin, which was her most treasured possession, and her coat, which might have kept her from freezing to death, but not her purse. Her cute little faux leather bag—along with her driver's license, credit and ATM cards, and a small amount of cash—was still in Ned's apartment.

She would have to go back.

No, she couldn't face him. Unless she went with the cop. She glanced over to where the police officer still sat, keeping a wary eye on her. No. She always kept a little emergency cash in the car. She would either go back later with Anne or just let it go. It would be a major hassle, but the cards could be replaced.

She opened the glove box and pulled out a crisp twenty-dollar bill. Then she locked the car, waved at the police officer and headed toward Walmart. A plow had cleared the lot during the night, so the pavement was mostly dry.

Her first stop was the bathroom. She gazed at her reflection in the mirror. Her hair was a mess and dark circles underlined her eyes. Her box of toiletries had also been abandoned at Ned's place, so she finger combed her hair the best she could, scrubbed at her teeth and rinsed her mouth with water. Feeling half way human, she walked toward the health and beauty section. She picked out a cheap toothbrush, small tube of paste, and a hairbrush. Then she headed to the registers, most of which were free at this hour of the morning. she grabbed a soda out of the refrigerator and a candy bar off the shelf. Breakfast.

The cashier, looking as bleary-eyed as Tori felt, rang up the small purchase. Tori paid, stuffed the woefully small amount of change in her jeans pocket, and returned to her car. The cop was gone. She started the engine and cranked up the heat. It had felt toasty warm inside the store, but she was still chilled. She ate the candy bar as her car heated up, and took slow sips of her soda. She glanced at her gas gauge. Half full. Good—she wouldn't need to get gas on the way to Anne's house.

She pulled onto the road. The plows had done their job and the roads seemed fine. That might change as she neared her destination, but she didn't anticipate any problem with the highway. She turned on the radio and tried not to think too much as she barreled on her way.

After about an hour, she exited the freeway. As she had expected, the smaller roads were rougher, but not too bad. Within twenty minutes, she drew up in front of Anne's house and parked the car. She sat for a moment, studying the small but cheerful house with its cozy front porch. It was still early. Anne wouldn't have left for work yet, but she wasn't expecting Tori until this afternoon. Tori sighed. *Might as well get it over with.*

She stepped out of the car, made her way up the walk, and rang the bell. A few moments later, a woman with long dark hair answered.

"Tori!" she said, surprise evident in her voice. "I wasn't expecting you so soon."

"I've run into a snag," Tori said, then all of a sudden she was crying, tears streaming down her face even as she tried to choke them down.

Anne didn't hesitate. "Come in." She grabbed Tori's arm and pulled her gently into the house. "Let's sit in the family room." She led Tori to the back of the house where a kids' show was playing on TV. Hannah, Anne's three-year-old daughter, lay on the floor with a pillow. She glanced up at her mother and Tori, but then turned her attention back to the show. "Sit down." Anne eased her into the plush sofa. Tori sank into its warmth, already feeling a bit better.

"Would you like something to drink?"

"Diet soda if you have it."

Anne frowned. "You know I don't drink that stuff. I'll make you some tea." She disappeared into the kitchen.

The couch was littered with throw pillows, and Tori placed one behind her back. All around her were objects either handmade by Anne or gleaned from antique shops. Lace doilies dotted the end and coffee tables. Original oil paintings hung from the walls. They weren't by famous artists and weren't even particularly well done, but the landscapes they depicted were raw and vibrant. Toys littered the floor and overflowed from baskets in the corners. It was a homey, lived-in look, completely unlike Ned's sterile apartment. It was even more welcoming than the sparsely decorated place she had shared with Stacy. She wondered what vibe Matt would bring to the space, but thinking of her duplicitous former roommate and boss made her angry, so she forced the thoughts away.

Anne returned with the tea. Hannah had been casting Tori glances out of the side of her eyes, but once her mother was back in the room, she relaxed. Anne placed the cups and a bowl of sugar on the coffee table. She spooned sugar into her own cup. "Do you take milk?"

Tori shook her head. She usually used artificial sweeteners, but she knew Anne wouldn't have any of those. She took a bit of sugar, and kept stirring the tea long after the granules had dissolved.

"Want to tell me about it?"

"I lost my job."

"No! But you're so good at what you do. I've never heard anyone play the violin quite like you."

"Oh, my musical ability wasn't in question; it was my people skills."

"Oh."

"No protest?" Tori lifted her brows.

"You can be a bit abrupt."

Tori shrugged. "I tell it like it is. I see little point in doing otherwise."

"Only when it comes to your music. You're perfectly easy to deal with in most situations, but become a perfectionist when you're wrapped up in your violin. People expect a certain degree of tact."

"It gets worse."

"Go on." Anne took a sip of her tea.

Tori did the same. "When I got home after cleaning out my office, Stacy had changed the locks on our apartment. She kicked me out so Matt, my former boss, could move in."

"You can't be serious."

"Deadly."

"Well, you're always welcome here."

Tori glanced around the comfortable room. Anne appeared to be doing okay, but she knew it couldn't be easy raising a daughter on the salary she made as a tour guide. "I don't want to be a burden."

"I don't know what would have happened to me and Hannah if it wasn't for your mom," Anne said.

"Well, I am going to take you up on that." Tori fell silent. Although her mom had been dead for over a year, it still hurt to talk about her. She had been a trained classical violinist, like Tori, but had gotten her practical nursing license and gone to work in the hospital after her husband deserted her, leaving her alone with a small child. Four years ago, Anne had been brought in to the emergency room already in advanced labor, with amnesia as a result of a head wound. Fortunately Hannah had been born safely, though it had been touch and go for both mother and child for awhile. Most of Anne's memory had returned as she recuperated, but she had never recalled the events directly leading up to Hannah's birth. She recalled running from an abusive lover, but thought she had fallen and hit her head. Regardless of how she had come to be injured, she had no one to turn to for help, a situation which resonated with Tori's mother. She had opened up her home to Anne and the baby after they were discharged from the hospital.

Hannah left her place on the floor and curled up in her mother's lap. She sucked on her thumb as she studied Tori with deep blue eyes.

Tori blinked and pushed the memories aside. "After Stacy threw me out, I needed some place to store my stuff because it wouldn't all fit in my car. My upstairs neighbor, Ned, offered to help. Do you remember Ned from my apartment complex? You met him at the swimming party."

"I think so. Tall guy?"

"Yes." Tori remembered him looming over her, pushing her against the wall. She took a deep breath. "We moved some of my things into his apartment. I was going to come down yesterday, but it was snowing and he said I could stay with him."

"Oh, no."

"He expected payment for his 'help.'"

"He didn't..."

"No, I got away. Those self-defense classes Mom made me take finally paid off." She fiddled with her hair. "I'm not sure he would have really gone through with it, but I was scared. I didn't do any permanent damage. Or at least, I don't think so."

"I hope you did."

"I'm in enough trouble without getting arrested."

"What can I do?"

"Well, I need a place to stay. Also, I left my purse at Ned's. We will have to go back and get it or I'll have to replace all my cards and my driver's license."

"I wouldn't mind getting my hands on him."

Tori actually laughed. "I just want my purse, Anne, although I appreciate the support."

Anne glanced at her watch. "No time to drive up this morning before my shift. Maybe tomorrow. We need to get going so I can drop Hannah off at daycare and get to work. You make yourself at home while I'm gone. You can put some of your stuff in Hannah's room. The rest will have to go in the basement."

Tori nodded, but she remembered Anne's basement, made of cinder blocks with a dirt floor, and wanted to avoid it if possible.

"Will you be okay to perform tonight? Do you even have your violin?"

"Of course."

"You remembered your violin, but not your purse?"

"Is that such a big surprise?"

"Guess not. What about your costume?"

"It's with my clothes in the car. Other than my purse, nothing at Ned's is critical."

"Okay. Well, I need to get dressed." Anne shifted Hannah to the floor. The little girl made a sound of protest and lifted her arms to be held again.

"Can Aunt Tori hold you so Mommy can get dressed?" Tori asked. She scooped the little girl up and sat back against the back of the couch, wincing at the pain in her head. Hannah stuck out her lower lip, but accepted the substitution. Tori didn't know much about toddlers, but Hannah had been an easy baby and seemed better behaved than most toddlers. As she held Hannah close, the horrors of the previous day began to fade away. Though she still worried about finding another job, at least she had a place to stay and someone who cared about her. Although Anne was not much older than Tori, motherhood had matured her and Tori had always looked up to her as she might a big sister.

When Anne returned she was dressed as a proper eighteenth century frontier woman in a long skirt and chemise, a long blouse that could double as a night shirt. She wore a bodice over the chemise. It was similar to Tori's costume for her gig. "Will you be all right?"

"Of course."

"Good." Anne gathered up her bags, which were already packed and waiting, and took Hannah's hand. "I get off at five."

The house seemed quiet once they were gone. Tori pulled her phone out of her pocket, glad she hadn't left it in her purse. She decided to check her email before beginning the task of hauling in her boxes. Maybe Matt had changed his mind and decided to rehire her. *And maybe I'll find a unicorn in the back yard.* She scrolled through her messages, skipping ones she wanted to come back to.

Cathy Peper

Soon her nearly sleepless night caught up with her, and she set the phone on the table, moved her pillow to the end of the couch, and slipped into a deep sleep.

Chapter 4

By the time Anne and Hannah returned, Tori had a pot of spaghetti simmering on the stove. If she was going to be sleeping on the couch, she figured she might as well make herself useful."

"You didn't have to do that," Anne said.

"I wanted to. Besides, it's not homemade. I'm not much of a cook."

"I'll give you some lessons while you're here." Anne stopped and shook her head. "Not that I'm expecting you to cook for us or anything." She bustled about setting the table and put Hannah in her booster seat. "It's bib night for you." She shot a look at Tori as she fastened an "I love Mommy" bib around her daughter's neck. "Spaghetti's a messy meal for a four-year-old."

"Didn't think about that." Tori dished out the pasta and placed a wedge of garlic bread on everyone's plate.

"Are you ready for tonight?" Anne asked once they had started eating.

Tori nodded. "I've been practicing the music for months and could probably play it in my sleep." She laughed without humor. "My constant practicing was one of the things that annoyed my roommate."

"I know a good word for Stacy, but can't say it in front of Hannah," Anne said.

"I appreciate your support. And thanks for getting me the gig, by the way. I knew the extra money would come in handy, but now it's critical."

"Too bad they don't do these parties year-round. You could give lessons here in Ste. Gen, but I don't think think there'd be enough students to make it worth your while."

"Maybe I could give lessons and get a part-time job doing something else."

"That might work, but you'd probably be looking at one of the larger nearby towns. There just aren't a lot of jobs here."

Tori wasn't surprised. Small towns struggled everywhere. She turned her attention back to her spaghetti. Hannah seemed to be enjoying it, but already her face was orange with sauce. When they finished eating, Tori went to put on her costume while Anne started the dishes. It was easy to pull on the chemise and skirt, and even the bodice laced up the front. Women on the frontier might have had a few servants, but they weren't the pampered ladies from back East—they had to be able to dress themselves without a maid. Tori tried to pile her hair on her head the way Anne wore hers to work, but her fine blond locks mutinied and kept slipping loose.

"Can you help me with my hair?"

"Certainly." Anne wiped her wet hands on a towel and came over. It took only a few minutes and a handful of bobby pins for her to tame Tori's unruly hair. "That should do it." She tilted her head to view her handiwork. "I think you look great—take a look."

Tori walked over to the mirror above the hall table. For a moment she scarcely recognized herself in the strange clothes and elegant hairstyle. Then the moment passed and she was just Tori, dressed for another performance, albeit slightly different than any she had ever given before. "Wow, it looks awesome and you made it seem easy."

"I've had lots of practice."

"True, it probably doesn't even seem strange for you to dress this way."

"Not really," Anne said dryly. "You remember which house you're going to?"

"Yeah. It's not very far, so I'll just walk over."

Anne frowned. "Normally I'd agree with you, but it looks like we're in for more snow. If you walk, be sure to bundle up."

"Yes, Mom."

Anne ignored her comment. "Do you have boots?"

Her boots had been in the coat closet in her apartment. Had she put that box in the car or left it with Ned? "Not sure. Let me check." She'd managed to stack everything against the wall in Hannah's room, avoiding the dank basement. She was used to more modern houses where the basements had concrete walls and floors. In Anne's older home, the basement was made of stone walls with a dirt floor.

She wandered into Hannah's very pink room and pulled a few boxes free, finding what she was looking for in the third box she checked. She found her sturdy fur-lined boots along with a jumble of shoes, jackets, hats, scarves, and gloves. She worried that replacing her ballet flats with her Ugg boots would ruin her elegant appearance, but was pleased to see they didn't show beneath her long skirt. She chose a hat, scarf and pair of heavy gloves as well before tossing the box back onto the pile, where it rested at a dangerous angle. Good enough. She needed to hurry if she was going to arrive early, as she had planned.

"I should be warm enough, but I don't look like a proper nineteenth-century woman anymore," she said as she slid her arms into her coat, wrapped a scarf around her neck, and stuffed a hat into her pocket. She wouldn't ruin Anne's handiwork by putting the hat on now, but it might come in handy on the way home.

"Oh, I don't know. Your outerwear isn't period, of course, and the materials are all wrong, but people had to dress warmly in those days if they wanted to survive. No central heating."

"True." Tori shivered at the thought. "Guess I'm ready." She tucked her shoes into her violin case.

"Wait." Anne was looking at her, a strange expression on her face.

"What? Do I have food stuck in my teeth?"

"I have a bad feeling about tonight." Anne, usually so composed, cracked her knuckles, then placed a hand against her forehead is if she had a headache.

Tori groaned. "Surely I've used up my share of bad luck. Anyway, this job is just for the month of December. Even if I get fired, I won't be that much worse off than I am now."

Anne waved her hand dismissively. "You won't get fired. I just don't like the look of the clouds."

"I'm not going to let a little snow daunt me." Tori pulled on her gloves.

"I think you need this." Anne reached for the chain around her neck.

Tori raised her brows. She had seen the pendant once before, when Anne first came to live with Tori and her mother. It was beautiful, with a deep blue stone and delicate silver-work. She'd glimpsed the chain numerous times throughout the years, so she knew her friend still wore the necklace, though she'd wondered why Anne kept it hidden. It wouldn't go with every outfit, of course, but it was lovely and obviously of sentimental value. "I can't. I know it's important to you."

"It is. My mother gave it to me before she died. She told me it had been passed down from mother to daughter for generations. After she gave it to me, she made me promise to always keep it close—but hidden. It's supposed to bring good fortune."

"See, you can't go breaking a promise you made to your mom."

"I think she would approve. If I'm wrong, you can always give it back to me."

"Well, of course I'll give it back to you. I'm just borrowing it for good luck tonight," Tori said as she reached for the necklace. "Are you sure? I'm fine, really; I'm not even nervous."

Anne nodded. "Wear it and be safe."

Tori smiled and slipped it over her head. "Thanks, Anne." To her surprise, Anne reached out and hugged her. Although they were close, neither of them was the hugging type. "I'll be back in a few hours."

"Yes—go, go." Anne shooed her out of the house. "Break a leg."

Tori stepped outside and glanced up at the sky. The clouds did look heavy—rather ominous, in fact. She hurried down the street, trying to decide if she had really seen the glint of tears in Anne's eyes or if it had just been a trick of the light.

Chapter 5

Anne lived close to the historic area, so a quick walk brought Tori to the Carpentier House, a well-preserved house built in the old French style, with vertical logs. A woman from the historical society let her in. "The musicians are in the parlor," she said, pointing to a room at the back of the house. "You can put your coat out on the back porch."

"Thanks," Tori said. She'd been to the house with Anne and knew her way around. It wasn't that large, anyway. She removed her coat and gloves on the porch and changed her shoes. Anne had delayed her enough that she wasn't the first musician to arrive, but only one other member of the quartet was there, the viola player. Though she had never played with this particular group before, Tori knew from Anne that the other members were two men and a woman. The other woman played the violoncello.

Tori greeted the viola player. He kept his bushy brown hair cropped short. She guessed him to be in his mid thirties, about a decade older than herself.

"I'm Danny," he said, sticking out his hand.

Tori shook it. He had a nice firm grip, but nothing showy. "Victoria, but most people call me Tori."

"Nice to meet you." He went back to tuning his instrument.

"Likewise." Tori set up her stand and placed her music on it. "Have you ever done one of these before?" She still didn't think the performance was that big a deal, but Anne's strange behavior had set her nerves on edge.

"I've been doing it for the last five years." He gave her a reassuring smile. "Don't worry. You'll be fine."

Tori smiled back and began her own tuning. The other two musicians, who were closer to Tori's age, arrived and soon the room was filled with the sounds of bows being dragged across strings. Danny quickly took charge, either because he was the oldest or because he had done this so many times. He explained to Tori that they were to provide background music as the guests mingled, ate, drank, and soaked up the atmosphere.

"The music, which you've already been given is either current for the time period or old favorites. We'll do them in this order."

Tori rearranged her music as he numbered the pieces, then took a sip of her hot apple cider, which was spiced with rum. The quartet had access to the full bar, and while she normally might have had a glass of wine, seeing the glass bottles had reminded her of Ned. She asked for water, but allowed herself to be talked into sampling the festive drink. She savored the sweet taste as the warmth and alcohol soothed her. Soon the first guests came in, stomping snow off their shoes, and Danny gave the group the signal to begin.

Tori lost herself in the music. She almost always did. Her audience, or lack thereof, didn't matter once she fell into familiar rhythms. After a period of adjustment, the group played well together, easily following Danny's lead. Although the house had been outfitted with central heating, a fire crackled in the hearth for atmosphere, and the drone of conversation provided a pleasing backdrop. If the words had been in French, instead of English, she might almost have felt she had traveled back in time to when the town had been part of the French empire.

After about an hour, they were given a break. Tori finished off her cider and then slipped away to the covered porch for some peace and quiet. The guests were allowed to go upstairs, but kept away from the porch and kitchen where caterers filled silver trays with period-inspired finger foods. The macarons, two meringue cookies stuck together with buttercream icing or jam, were her favorites, even though Anne had told her that serving them in that way was an anachronism. She had done some research into French cooking and although macarons had been brought to France from Italy in the 1500's, they were not served together with filling until the 1830's, about forty years after the time period they were portraying tonight. She snatched a couple of the desserts, along with a slice of ham, rolled and secured with a toothpick, from a passing waiter and carried her snack to the porch railing. Originally the kitchen had been detached from the main building, but the addition of the porch and a short hallway now gave covered access to the house. Although covered and screened off, the porch was unheated and Tori could see her breath.

As Anne had feared, it was snowing again, harder than yesterday. Tori watched the frenzy for a moment from the shelter of the porch, then following a crazy impulse, pushed the screen door open and stepped out into the yard. Flakes settled upon her clothes and covered her hair and eyelashes. Like a child, she stuck out her tongue and tasted them. Cold and rough, the snow melted in her mouth. Shivering, she turned to go, but a flicker of light caught her eye. *Was that lightning?* She looked in the direction of the light and it came again, arcing across the sky like it was a hot summer night rather than a cold winter one.

Spooked as well as chilled, she hurried up the snow-covered steps, stomping her feet once she got back on the porch to shake loose the snow. Her feet ached from the cold. Going outside had probably not been the best decision. Her feet would be cold and wet the rest of the night.

She picked up another hot cider on her way back to her chair in the parlor. Her fellow musicians were also returning, armed with fresh drinks. Tori straightened her music and scanned the crowd. A handful of couples had gotten into the spirit and wore period costumes similar to Tori's, but most of the guests sported typical black tie attire—suits and cocktail dresses. Space was limited in the house and tickets for the weekend Christmas parties were pricey. Participants tended to be well-to-do or true history fanatics. She wasn't paying much attention, but a familiar couple made her stop and stare.

It can't be! But it was. The parents of Jason, her lazy, nonpracticing violin student, were here, Mr. and Mrs. Henderson. Fate must really have it in for her. She closed her eyes. Unfortunately, when she opened them, the Hendersons were still there.

They wouldn't notice her. She was just a member of the quartet, one of the help, practically a stick of furniture. But then Mrs. Henderson grabbed her husband's arm and whispered into his ear. Mr. Henderson looked right at Tori, a sneer marring his classic features.

Oh oh. They recognized her. Hopefully they wouldn't want to cause a scene at a fancy affair. They had already gotten her fired from one job; wasn't that enough?

It seemed as though, perhaps it was. Although Mrs. Henderson had been the one to point her out, she tugged on her husband's arm and tried to draw him away. Mr. Henderson's expression remained grim, but some of the red faded from his face and he allowed his wife to steer him toward the stairs. Tori sighed, feeling as if she'd been paroled. Her hands shook as she picked up her violin, and she hoped she would still be able to play.

Danny gave the signal and they began. Tori hit a sour note, wincing as Danny glared at her. She gritted her teeth and concentrated, trying to forget the Hendersons. To a degree, she succeeded: She made no further errors and, although she couldn't lose herself in the music as she had before, Danny seemed satisfied with her performance.

The second half seemed much longer than the first, but at last it was over. The woman from the historical society, who was in charge of the evening, made an announcement as everyone was preparing to leave.

"It's snowing much harder than expected. We already have close to six inches. Those of you planning to return to St. Louis tonight might want to reconsider. All the rooms in Ste. Genevieve were probably booked months ago, but the nearby towns have empty rooms. If you want to stay, I can help you find a place." Some of the couples drifted towards the organizer.

Tori felt grateful that Anne had made her wear her boots. Her feet had never fully recovered from their earlier exposure. She packed up her supplies and made her way to the porch. Dressed for the elements, she slipped out the back door. She struggled to open the back gate which had a half-foot of snow already piled up against it, but a hard shove did the job. The street was quiet and free of people, since most everyone had left by the front door. The eerie lightning still flashed across the sky, and she heard thunder rumble in the distance. Shivering, although she wasn't truly cold, Tori struck out for Anne's house.

She had walked less than a block when a man stepped from the shadows. "Call my son a liar, huh?" His voice was slightly slurred, as if he'd had too much to drink.

"Mr. Henderson." Tori's breath caught in her throat. "Please, it's late. I never meant to cause any harm."

"Then you should watch your mouth."

"I only said Jason needs to practice more often if he truly wants to learn to play the violin."

"According to my wife, you said he doesn't practice at all, but Jason assures us that he completes his lessons every day."

Liar! There, now she'd thought it, even if she hadn't said it. "Perhaps I spoke too hastily. Jason's progress makes it seem like he's not practicing, but I could be wrong about that."

The man in front of her paused and seemed to consider her words. Tori hoped that, in his inebriated state, he wouldn't realize she had just accused his son of being slow, or at least slow at learning the violin, if his claims of practicing were to be believed. "I listened to you tonight. You play all right, but you shouldn't be teaching children."

"Well, thanks to you, I'm not. Now please let me by. We both need to get out of this weather." She wondered if he was driving back to St. Louis or staying in a nearby hotel. He was in no condition to drive, even without the snow.

"Hoity-toity little bitch." Thunder rumbled.

Tori gasped. Giving him a wide berth, she tried to pass. *Not wide enough.* He grabbed her arm and yanked her close, his sour breath filling her nostrils. Panic bloomed and the memory of Ned's behavior filled her head. "Let go of me!" Where was his wife? Where were her fellow musicians and the other guests? It seemed as if she and Mr. Henderson were alone, the snow that covered the street blanketing all sound.

"Apologize to my wife."

"Fine. Take me to her." Tori felt a prickle of heat on her breast bone. The necklace Anne had lent her warmed against her skin, and she took comfort in its presence.

"You're not worth it." He shoved her away, hard enough that she slipped and fell in a heap. He tromped back toward the house, slipping and nearly falling himself. A particularly bright bolt of lightning lit the sky, followed by a echoing boom.

Tori picked herself up and brushed the snow off her backside. It was still coming down so fast that it was mostly a hopeless task. Just in the few minutes it had taken for Mr. Henderson to berate and assault her, her clothes had become covered. She shook with reaction. *What on earth is wrong with that man? Or do all men just have it out for me?* Her breath came quick and shallow as she trudged through the snow, eager for the safety and warmth of Anne's house.

A few minutes later she stopped and brushed the snow from her eyes. She didn't recognize the buildings squatting in front of her. She must have taken a wrong turn. Nothing looked the same buried in the snow, with only the weak glow of the streetlights and the flashes overhead to light the way. Her heart pounded. What if Mr. Henderson had followed her? He could kill her and no one would ever know. All he had to do was toss her body into the river...

The river. She could smell it. Even hear the soft slapping of its water against the dock. Somehow she had gone toward the river instead of away. It had been foolish to panic. All she had to do was turn around. Instead, she walked forward. Now that she had her bearings, she recognized a few of the shops along Main Street. Leaving them behind, she wandered closer to the water, seeming almost drawn to it.

The Mississippi chugged slow and deep. On the far bank was Illinois. For a moment, as lightning tore a hole in the sky, she almost thought she could see it. Thunder rocked the ground where she stood. The river beckoned, silent and mysterious, as something warm hummed against her chest. Tori reached for the necklace Anne had lent her, reassured once again by its presence, but wondering why it felt so hot. Grateful as she was for Anne's kindness, the necklace had not manifested good luck. Mr. Henderson would probably talk to the historical society and she'd be out of yet another job.

She tugged the necklace free from all her layers. It was hot to the touch, perhaps from absorbing the heat of her skin. But the blue crystal, already striking in its intensity, appeared to glow. It hadn't been glowing when Anne gave it to her. Light flashed overhead and the stone pulsed in sync. *This is getting too weird.* As she turned to go, a car came around the corner, headlights glaring. The driver leaned on his horn and the loud noise cut through the dark. She stepped back as the car slid toward her and her feet lost purchase on the slippery slope. She fell again, but farther and faster this time, toward the inky depths of the river. She screamed, the sound swallowed by a crack of thunder. Lightning lit the riverbank bright as day for an endless second. Her necklace popped and shimmered, and then the icy waters of the Mississippi closed over her head.

Chapter 6

St. Louis, Missouri
December 1811

Wearing fur-lined gloves but no coat, Sebastien La Roche labored alongside his employees, filling his boat with furs, barrels of dried corn, and other produce bound for the market at New Orleans. Their mood was buoyant, laughter and curses flying in equal measure as they stored their cargo and supplies for the dangerous but relatively easy trip downriver. It was coming back up, dragging the boat foot by painful foot against the current, that gave the keelboat operators their boasting, boisterous reputation. No one else on the river could touch them for sheer strength or courage, and they knew it well.

They didn't fill the hold; they'd stop in Ste. Genevieve and New Madrid to offload some of their goods and take on more. Now that fur trapping had moved farther west as Missouri's beaver population declined, Sebastien had nearly abandoned trapping for trading on the river. He still owned a small cabin in Colorado where he and his father had spent many a winter trapping game and stockpiling furs, but he considered St. Louis his home. He had kept a room in a boarding house there ever since his father's death, when the house where he had grown up had passed to his stepmother.

"That should do it," said Roger, his second-in-command.

"Set a pair of men to guard it. We leave on the morrow."

Roger nodded. "Off to see your stepmother?"

"Not by choice, but I feel some degree of obligation to her."

"I wouldn't. Not after what she did to your sister."

Sebastien compressed his lips. "What happened to Ari was as much my fault as Martha's."

"Like hell! She's a cold woman and doesn't deserve your kindness."

Sebastien gave a bark of laughter, but there was no humor in it. "Don't worry. She won't receive any kindness from me, old friend." He strode down the gangplank to the muddy shore. St. Louis wasn't much of a town compared to New Orleans or the cities he had heard of back East, but with its position on the Mississippi he thought it would continue to prosper. A couple of major streets ran parallel to the river, while several others ran perpendicular. His childhood home was on one of the side streets and it didn't take him long to walk over there and bang on the door. When his stepmother opened it, she frowned.

"Sebastien," she said, stepping back to allow him entrance.

"Martha." He entered the house, noting that although the rooms were the same, and even much of the furniture, the place looked, smelled, and felt different than when his mother had lived there. The kitchen out back held no welcoming stew simmering over the fire, nor did the sweet, yeasty smells of baking permeate the air. Though she had made an effort while his father was alive, Martha considered cooking an onerous chore, to be relegated to someone else if possible. The parlor and dining room were neat, but bare of flowers.

"I'm off again. I've brought your allowance. Spend it wisely. Depending on what we find in New Orleans, this just might be the time I decide to take the *Fury* out east." With every trip he made downriver, he was tempted to go up the Ohio on his return. He knew he could get a good price for his goods at Pittsburgh, but it was a longer journey and he didn't know the waters of the Ohio as well as he knew the Mississippi.

Martha looked unconcerned. "You never do."

"There's always a first time."

"You will do whatever makes you the most money."

He wondered why he allowed her to get under his skin. "My cargo will fetch more if I go to Pittsburgh."

Martha shrugged. "Then why don't you?"

"It would take longer." *And there is more risk.*

"Your father couldn't understand your desire for profit. It broke his heart when you became more interested in trading than trapping."

His stepmother wasn't telling him anything he didn't already know. "I'll go out to the cabin next year. Game is growing ever more scarce. Soon not even Colorado will be far enough away."

"River or wilderness, it matters not to me so long as you remember your responsibility to your father's widow."

"I'm not sure why I should, when you didn't remember your responsibility to your husband's children."

Martha dropped her gaze, unable to meet his eyes. "I made a mistake. One I will regret forever."

Sebastien knew he would never forgive himself for his sister's death, either.

"Women die in childbirth. It happens all the time. Even in the best of circumstances," Martha said.

Yes, but how much more likely was it for a woman to die under unfavorable circumstances? "Do you have any special requests? No guarantees, of course, but something I might be able to pick up in New Orleans?"

Bringing home rare luxuries had been one of his favorite parts of heading down river when his father had first given in to his pleas to expand their business. Father and son had bought a flatboat, taken it to New Orleans to sell their cache of furs, and walked home. They hadn't been able to carry much with them, but Sebastien had brought home a vial of perfume for his mother—his real mother, not the dour woman standing before him. He knew his father had been lonely when his wife died, but Sebastien never could understand why he had married Martha. She was pretty enough, he supposed, for a middle-aged woman. And women were hard to come by on the frontier, but still she was nothing like his cheerful mother.

"Just come home safely."

Sebastien nodded as he turned to go. The woman was a piece of work. He could almost imagine that she cared for his welfare rather than his sporadic support payments.

* * *

Sebastien arrived at his boat early the next morning, eager to begin his journey. Roger met him on shore and drew him aside.

"Some of the furs disappeared overnight."

"How is that possible? I told you to have the boat watched."

"I did. I set Hank and Arnie on it, both good men. They swear they never left their post, but somehow those furs walked."

Sebastien scowled. It wasn't the first time some of his cargo had gone missing. Pirates roamed the river, luring unwary boatmen ashore only to murder the crew and steal the boat. Bands of Indians sometimes attacked, killing or capturing the crew and making off with as much cargo as they could carry. He was wise to pirate tricks, never picking up people "stranded" on shore, and had been lucky enough to avoid Indian attacks—so far. He also had yet to lose a boat to the hazards of the river, although he'd been grounded a time or two. All in all, he'd been quite lucky, but the trickle of stolen goods annoyed him. Much as he hated to suspect one of his crew, it was looking more and more likely that the theft was an inside job. "It must be one of the men. Be on the look out."

"Aye, I will." Roger sounded as weary as Sebastien felt.

"We'd best push off. Is the Rattler ready to go?" Sebastien always traveled with at least one other keelboat for mutual protection. This time he had paired off with a cocky braggart who styled himself Bob "the Rattler" Rivers. It wasn't unusual for keelers to take on nicknames. Sebastien himself was known as "Eagle Eyes" in some circles, for his skill in spotting obstacles in the river.

Bob seemed like a decent enough fellow—fairly new to western waters, but with a good track record. Sebastien had his doubts whether Bob Rivers was any more the man's given name than "the Rattler", but he didn't care. If Bob was running from something, let him run. Trouble tended to run a man to ground in the end, unless he changed his ways. Sebastien couldn't bring himself to trust the man, but as long as the Rattler kept his fangs sheathed, Sebastien would let him be.

"They've been stirring for a while, but I'll go find out," Roger said. He crossed over to the other vessel, calling for the *patron*, or captain. For all that Roger was old for the keelboat trade, he never shirked his duties. The backbreaking labor of poling the boats upstream made it a young man's job, but what Roger lacked in brawn, he made up for in experience. Besides, he'd been with Sebastien from the beginning, had invested his own savings into the enterprise and was more friend than employee.

The sun peeked over the horizon by the time they left port, and the ominous blaze of the comet—which had plagued the region since fall—faded in the morning light. Many of the crew took it as a bad omen, and although Sebastien wasn't particularly superstitious, it made him uneasy as well. River travel was dangerous enough without fiery objects threatening to fall from the sky.

The weather was fairly mild for December, and the water high enough to make their passage swift and uneventful. It was during the dry season that the pitfalls lurking just beneath the surface snagged the careless navigator and made some parts of the river virtually impassable. Fallen trees, with their roots stuck to the muddy bottom of the river, lurked just beneath the water's surface, waiting to pierce the hull of a passing boat. Sandbars built up, shrinking and growing as the current shifted. No matter how well a captain knew the river, he had to be prepared for change.

They made good time to Ste. Genevieve, but as they drew closer to shore in preparation for docking, Sebastien caught sight of something in the water that didn't belong. To his horror, he realized it was a body. Since they were so close to town and not in a place pirates usually operated, he didn't think it was a trick. He called for a stop and ordered the men to paddle closer to the victim. It was a woman. Long fair hair floated around her pale face and she wore a strange, blue, padded coat.

"Pull her in!" he yelled. The men obeyed, grabbing her and dumping her on the deck as Sebastien jumped down from his post atop the cabin and hurried toward them.

Between the treacherous currents and the winter cold, he knew there was little chance she was still alive, but either way he had to take her to Ste. Genevieve where the sheriff could handle the matter. He would determine whether she had gone into the water dead or alive and try to search out whomever was responsible.

As he approached, Sebastien's men dropped back and gave him access. She couldn't have been in the water long. There were no signs of damage or decay on her still features. She was beautiful, even with her hair wet and straggly and her unusual, masculine-looking waterlogged coat. A pretty and possibly valuable necklace hung from her neck. It might provide a clue to her identity if no one recognized her. Sebastien wiped a tendril of tangled hair from her face. To his astonishment, she moaned and her eyes fluttered open, and he found himself staring into blue eyes surrounded by dark lashes. She was alive.

* * *

Tori looked up into fierce, deep-set blue eyes. Before she could do more than process that the face they belonged to was handsome as well, the stranger swept her up in his arms and yelled something incomprehensible to someone behind him. Confused, she struggled in his grasp, but her efforts did her no good. She was cold, colder than she had ever been in her life, and dripping wet. What on earth had happened? Her memory was a little fuzzy, but the last thing she recalled was the icy cold waters of the Mississippi closing over her head. No wonder she was cold and wet. It was December, not a good time to swim in the Big Muddy.

The man carried her into a small room made almost entirely of wood, kicked the door shut behind him, and laid her on a narrow cot. Tori shook uncontrollably.

He muttered something else, but she couldn't distinguish the words. He seemed to be speaking a foreign language. He fumbled with her clothes, pulling her skirt off, but seemed stymied by her coat, which was too tight to pull over her head.

"Stop," she rasped, slapping at his hands. "What do you think you're doing?" Her voice sounded strange to her ears and it hurt to speak.

The man narrowed his eyes at her. "We pulled you from the river. You must get out of these wet clothes before you freeze to death."

This time she understood him. "I can do it."

The man gave her a dubious look, but stepped back. "Very well. This is my cabin." He lifted the lid of a wooden trunk to display a stash of clothes. "You can borrow whatever you need. I'll be right outside."

Tori waited until she heard the sound of the door closing, then unzipped her down coat with shaking hands. Why had her rescuer tried to pull it over her head? Her bodice, shift, bra and panties followed her coat into a pile on the floor. Water weighted down her Uggs and she pulled them off, too, along with her wool socks. Grabbing the first item of clothing from the trunk, she toweled herself dry.

It didn't seem much warmer in the cabin than outside, but at least she was out of her wet clothes. From the motion beneath her feet, she guessed she was on some sort of boat. She dug through the rest of the items in the trunk. As she had expected, there was nothing that fit her. The man seemed to live in a collection of red flannel shirts and strange looking leather pants. Knowing the pants would never stay up, she donned one of the shirts, sighing at the warmth provided by the thick, soft material. She searched through the rest of the trunk, but if he had any boxers or briefs, they must be packed away somewhere else. She felt uncomfortable going commando, but guessed she had no choice for now. She did uncover a pair of socks, which she pulled over her icy feet. Then she pushed the door open a crack.

The man opened it the rest of the way. "You look much better," he said.

Tori nodded, although the hem of his shirt reached her knees and the garment hung on her slim frame. Shivers continued to wrack her body and she suspected she looked a mess. "You saved my life. Thank you."

"How did you end up in the river?"

Tori's head hurt as she tried to remember. There had been a bright light and a loud noise—a memory teased at her brain. "I fell during the thunderstorm."

The man frowned. "What thunderstorm?"

"From last night—you must have heard it." *Unless it was localized.*

His frown deepened, but he didn't argue with her. "You may have hit your head. Are you sure no one pushed you into the river?"

A shiver slid down her spine. "I don't think so. He was angry, but there was snow on the ground and it was slippery."

"Who was angry?"

"The man. It was dark... I think it was Mr. Henderson."

"If someone hurt you, you need to let the law know."

"I don't want to press any charges. I just want to go home. Can you tell me where I am?"

"We will be pulling into Ste. Genevieve momentarily. We found you floating just above town. Do you live here?"

"Not exactly." She rubbed her temples. Suddenly she gasped, remembering that she had been carrying her violin. "Did you find anything else with me?"

"Like what?"

"A violin."

"No, but the river might have carried it downstream."

"I don't suppose it would be damaged anyway, if it got wet." She drew air into her lungs, trying to stave off panic. She would have to replace it, of course. She had no way to make a living without it. But not having her well-loved instrument by her side made her feel more naked than being without underwear.

"You still look cold. Let me get you a fur. We will take you ashore in a few minutes."

"Thank you." She tried to dredge up a smile. "Your pants didn't fit."

"I suppose they would not." He returned the smile which made him look younger. "I'll be right back."

Chapter 7

Tori sat on the lumpy bunk and hoped that her handsome, burly savior would hurry with the promised furs. It was cold in the cramped cabin and it wouldn't surprise her if she was suffering from hypothermia. She was having difficulty remembering what had happened. It had been snowing. And the man, Mr. Henderson, her student's father, had yelled at her.

Had he pushed her? Surely not. He might be an overprotective parent, but he wasn't crazy. She could have drowned. You don't kill your child's music teacher just because you don't like her methods. Then she remembered the car. She hadn't been able to see who was behind the wheel. It could have been Henderson. Had the car really tried to run her down? She'd been upset, disoriented...she wasn't sure.

There had been lightning and thunder. In a snowstorm? She must be getting confused. And her necklace had glowed in the dark. *Now I'm really going off the deep end.* But everything seemed so strange. The man who had rescued her had addressed her in a foreign language—French, she thought, though she couldn't be sure. He'd switched to English easily enough, but why speak in French at all? Even in English, he spoke with an accent that curled her toes and made her think of wine and chocolate. He wore leather pants, a red shirt, and a leather jacket hung with fringe. He looked like he'd stepped out of a history book. And his boat was unlike anything she had ever seen before. She'd been too cold and frightened to notice much while on deck, but the cabin was made all of wood—wooden floor, wooden walls; no plastic anywhere in sight. He kept his clothes in a heavy antique trunk instead of a convenient duffel bag. Could he and his buddies be part of some kind of re-enactment group? Hysteria rose as she recalled how he'd seemed confused by her down jacket.

A quick knock heralded the man's return. It took him only a few strides to cross the narrow space and wrap an animal hide around her shoulders. That's what it certainly appeared to be—the skin of some poor animal removed for its fur. Tori hunkered gratefully into its warmth even though a faint musky odor clung to it.

The boat lurched as if it had run aground. Tori nearly fell off the bed, but the Frenchman braced himself with legs spread wide and merely laughed. "We've arrived. Can you put your boots back on? It's far too cold for stockinged feet."

Tori nodded, although sticking her feet back into her sodden boots made her flinch.

"Forgive me, I never introduced myself. "I'm Sebastien La Roche, captain of the *Fury*."

"The fury?"

"My boat." He was looking at her expectantly.

Oh, she needed to tell him who she was, even if everything seemed a bit fuzzy. "I'm Tori, Tori Foster."

"Tory?" He rolled the syllables in his mouth. "An unusual name to be sure."

"It's short for Victoria."

"A nickname, as I am sometimes called Eagle Eyes."

Eagle Eyes? Tori decided to let it go. Soon she would be safe with Anne and this strange encounter would seem like a dream.

"I will take you ashore now," he said and plucked her off the cot as if she weighed nothing.

"I can walk," she protested.

"I will set you down on dry land. You should not get wet again today."

Tori found herself glad for the help when she realized they were moored to a street. There was no dock; the men walked down a gangplank to reach the shore. Sebastien carried her easily and deposited her on the road. The dirt road. An older man approached them and said something to Sebastien that she couldn't understand.

"She's American," Sebastien replied in English. "She seems a bit muddled as to where she's from and how she got in the river."

Of course I'm American. This was America, what else would I be? Well, she supposed she could have been a foreign tourist, but really, what were the odds of that?

"Poor lass." The man patted her on the back like she was a stray dog.

"I thought we were at Ste. Genevieve," she said. The handful of buildings along the road looked familiar, but the town seemed much smaller than it should be, only a handful of streets which, from her position, appeared to be no more than dirt tracks.

Sebastien looked confused. "We are. We will have you situated in no time."

Tori caught her lip in her teeth. She'd had a traumatic experience. She might be in shock or even in a coma. This might all be a weird dream. Yes, she'd fallen, struck her head and now lay in the nearest hospital in a coma, dreaming of hunky French frontiersmen. She took a shallow breath. She hadn't traveled into the past. Time travel was impossible. *Isn't it?*

She followed her rescuers up to the row of buildings. Her feet ached with cold in her water-logged boots. If she was going to have a coma dream, why couldn't it have taken place on a tropical beach? Sebastien steered her toward one of the larger buildings. When she stepped inside, she saw it was a shop. Small to the eyes of someone used to malls and huge box stores, the compact space displayed a wide variety of items: bolts of cloth, dishes and cookware, sewing notions, cute little shoes made of leather, and even a porcelain doll tucked away in a corner.

> 53

A man stood behind the counter and Sebastien greeted him as if they were well—acquainted. Soon they were deep in discussion about items Sebastien could provide to the little store, and goods that the shop owner might sell to Sebastien for him to dispose of in New Orleans. Not particularly interested in this, Tori wandered over to examine the shelves. She didn't think she had ever been in this particular building, but she had toured some of the historic structures with Anne. If she remembered correctly, the tourist attraction looked similar to this shop, with one room for merchandise and the other rooms for the use of the family. She wondered if the owners of this store also lived on the premises.

"Victoria," Sebastien called. She returned to his side. "Do you know Mr. Mason?"

She glanced at the shopkeeper. He looked very formal in a heavy dark coat and white shirt, like he'd just stepped from an oil painting. "I don't believe so."

"Have you ever seen Miss Foster? We found her in the river. Whatever misfortune led to her being there seems to have damaged her memory. I thought she might be from town."

"I've never seen her before and I know most everyone who lives here. She must have come from an outlying farm."

"I see." Sebastien shot her a dubious look. "Have you remembered anything else? Do you think you live on a farm?"

Tori felt like laughing. She had always lived in the suburbs and knew next to nothing about farming. "I don't think—no, I'm sure I don't live on a farm." She was tired, hungry, and aching in every limb. Somehow it all seemed too real and too uncomfortable to be a dream. And it was far too elaborate to be a hoax. It seemed best to pretend to even more confusion than she actually felt until she could understand what was happening.

Mr. Mason gave her a sympathetic look. "Best take her to the church."

Another group of men, dressed similarly to Sebastien, entered the store. Their leader, a man who walked with the same lanky confidence as Sebastien, began bartering with Mr. Mason. He looked vaguely familiar, and Tori realized he was the from the other boat that had docked with them.

"Come." Sebastien led her out of the shop. "Wait here. I need to give my men some instructions and then I will take you to the church."

"Why?"

"The priests will know what to do with you."

Tori didn't like the sound of that. She didn't want to be separated from Sebastien who had not only saved her life, but also shown her a rough kindness. If her suspicions were true—if she had somehow traveled back in time—she was not only out of her element but also, as a woman, nearly devoid of rights. "Please don't abandon me."

"I'd like to get you back where you belong, but you don't seem to know where that is."

Tori wished he could get her back as well, but somehow she didn't think he could help her return to the twenty-first century. "You found me by the river. That means I must belong near the river."

"Fine. Come with me. Maybe you will remember something. But then I will take you to the church. We won't be here more than a day or two and I can't take you with me."

Tori followed Sebastien back to the *Fury*. There were no cars, no paved roads. A man passed them on a horse and tipped his old-fashioned hat to them. Even the river looked different. It seemed wider and wilder. The banks had been cleared near the town, but even from where she stood she could see the forest encroaching on the waterway, brush growing right up to its sides. There were other craft on the water—keelboats, such as the *Fury*, and square-shaped flat boats. But she saw none of the huge barges that plied the water in her own time, nor even the brightly painted steamboats that she had seen carrying passengers for a nostalgic day trip near the Gateway Arch.

She waited while Sebastien gave orders to the older man who seemed to have a position of some authority. Then he went back on the boat and emerged carrying a satchel. "I've put your wet clothes in here," he said.

Tori had forgotten how inappropriately dressed she was. Fortunately the large fur covered most of her. "What day is it?" she asked Sebastien as they walked back to town.

"It's December. The fifth, I think. Have you remembered something?"

She ignored his question for the moment. "What year?" she asked, holding her breath.

He gave her a strange look. "Why, 1811, of a certainty. I see how you might have lost a few days, but to forget the year? How can this be?"

Tori struggled to improvise. "I think I was on a boat. But then I fell off. Yes, I fell off and hit my head." She was flustered, trying to come up with a plausible story that wouldn't get her committed to a mental institution. But something about the year bothered her, something she might be able to dredge out of her memory if she had time to think.

She wasn't given that luxury. "And no one tried to rescue you?" Sebastien asked, looking suspicious.

"I don't think anyone realized what had happened. By now they are probably frantic." Tori was starting to enjoy the idea of a boat filled with people worrying about her.

Sebastien, however, appeared less than convinced. "Maybe Father Andre will know where you belong."

I doubt that. Still, she followed Sebastien for she had no where else to go. She had visited the Catholic church in her time—a lovely building made of red brick with a tall, elegant steeple soaring toward the sky—so she had not expected to be confronted with a simple vertical-log building. "That's the church?" she asked in disbelief. She recalled Anne telling her the church had been rebuilt on the same site once it became too small to serve the residents, but this must be an even earlier version.

"It's built in the French tradition. Perhaps you are more accustomed to horizontal log construction?"

"That must be it." She stepped into the primitive little church, squinting at the sudden darkness. The priest must have heard them, as he left the altar and ambled in their direction.

He inclined his head as he reached them and said something in French.

"My men and I found this young lady in the river. She thinks she fell from a boat, but can't recall all the details. I was wondering if you knew her." Sebastien spoke in English.

The priest studied her with dark, solemn eyes. "I've never seen her before."

The priest's accent was heavier than Sebastien's, but Tori found herself amazed by how easily everyone she had met appeared to switch from one language to another. "I told you I fell from a boat."

"You might still have been local, or have visited Ste. Genevieve previously."

"Are you bound for New Orleans?" Father Andre asked Sebastien.

"Yes. Can she stay here? I have no room for her on the keelboat."

"I can arrange for her to stay somewhere in town, but if she has no means to pay, she would be expected to work for room and board."

"I could take her on to New Madrid, but again, where would she stay? If someone is willing to house her here, I could pick her up on my way home and take her to St. Louis where she might be able to find work."

Find work? In nineteenth-century America? Doing what? Annoyed that the two men seemed content to plan her future without even consulting her, she fumed silently. *Hold your tongue. You are in unfamiliar territory.* But really, what could she do except play the

> 57

violin. The hunger she had felt earlier slipped into nausea. Her only ability lay in her music. Of course, she was literate—a skill that not everyone, and certainly not every woman—possessed in this time period. "I can read and write," she blurted out.

The priest narrowed his gaze at her. "An unusual skill. Cooking and cleaning would serve you better."

"I don't think she's from the servant class." Sebastien reached for her hand, turned it palm up, and showed it to Father Andre. "No calluses."

Except on my fingers. "I play the violin."

If anything, the priest looked even more disapproving. "She must have come from the East."

"I had the same thought."

"You should take her on to New Orleans. From there she can take a ship back to her home."

Sebastien's brows drew together. "I don't take passengers, Father. You know that."

"No one will be willing to shelter her for months without some form of compensation."

"I will pay a nominal room and board if someone will keep her until my return," Sebastien said shortly.

Tori thought he sounded angry. No doubt she would feel the same in his position, forced to support a stranger he had already wrested from death. She wanted to beg Sebastien to reconsider taking her to New Orleans. She didn't want to be an unwanted guest for months. But it all seemed like too much effort. The lingering fragrance of incense hung in the air, making it difficult to breathe. The candlelight, already low, dimmed further, and the cold, which had plagued her ever since she had regained consciousness on the deck of the *Fury*, vanished in a swirl of heat. She couldn't speak, see or breathe. But she realized she could still feel when she collapsed upon the smooth planks of the floor.

Chapter 8

One moment Victoria was standing next to him; the next, she had fainted and fallen to the floor. Sebastien knelt and drew her into his arms for the third time that day. She fit easily there, slim and long-legged. She was taller than he had originally surmised, taller even than some men he knew. But she was slender, and years of propelling a keelboat up the river had given him rock-hard muscles. "Where's the doctor?" he asked Father Andre who stood gaping at him like a fish.

"Doctor?"

"She has taken ill from being in the water. I should have expected as much. You do have a doctor in town?"

"Yes, we do." The priest seemed to have regained his poise. "Follow me." He grabbed a thick woolen cloak from a peg on the wall, threw it around his shoulders and strode down the street. He stopped in front of a house with a sign hanging out front. The sign bore a picture of a winged staff with two snakes twining around it. He strode up the steps and banged on the door.

A pink-cheeked young woman answered, gasping as she saw Victoria. "Bring her in. I will get the doctor." Sebastien laid Victoria down on the table in the center of the room.

"Doctor!" the woman yelled. "We have a patient."

A man hurried down the stairs. A pair of spectacles perched on his nose, while tufts of white hair stuck out all over his balding head. "What's wrong with her?"

"Isn't that your job?" Sebastien snapped.

The doctor shot him a none-too-friendly look. "Explain to me what happened so I can give the proper diagnosis."

For what seemed like the hundredth time, Sebastien explained how he had rescued Victoria from the river, how she had been deeply chilled, and how she had seemed confused about how she had gotten there and even basic information, like the year. As he spoke the doctor looked down her throat, lifted her eyelids and peered inside, and placed a mirror to her mouth to make certain she was still breathing. "I guess that explains why she is dressed so strangely," he said when Sebastien finished.

Sebastien had forgotten that she was wearing his borrowed shirt. "Her clothes were soaked. My shirt was the best we could do."

"Clear the room, May. Let me see to the patient."

Sebastien and Father Andre followed May from the room. "I will see if I can find somewhere for her to stay," the priest said before taking his leave.

Sebastien hesitated. He wasn't sure why. He had done all he could for her and she was in good hands. "Will she be all right?" he asked May.

"Dr. Bennett was educated back East. She will receive the best care."

The words were not as comforting as Sebastien would have liked. He wasn't sure why it mattered. He'd known the woman less than a day. "I can be reached at my boat, if needed."

"I wouldn't worry," May said. "She seems strong, and if she pulls through I don't think she will be without a home for long. A girl who looks as she does... someone will take her to wife."

He should have been relieved. The last thing he needed was another woman to be responsible for. He gave May a polite nod and headed back to the *Fury*. While his men were on shore imbibing at the tavern and kicking up larks, he planned to stay on board and make certain no more of his cargo disappeared.

* * *

Tori felt hot and cold by turns. She lay on a comfortable bed, wrapped in warm blankets, but her bones and muscles felt as if she had been trampled at an out-of-control rock concert. She knew from the heat of her skin that fever raged through her body, and her mind felt clouded and unclear. Something momentous had happened, but she couldn't quite remember what. She didn't recognize the man or woman who were caring for her. *Am I in a hospital?* It didn't seem like she was. The room, although equally unfamiliar, looked like someone's bedroom, not the utilitarian starkness of a hospital room. And she wasn't hooked up to any monitors or an IV.

She wondered if Anne knew where she was and that she was sick. She hoped her friend would visit, and she also longed for the sight of a handsome but scruffy young man whose name she could not recall. Was he her boyfriend? Somehow she didn't think so.

The woman came and went at regular intervals. She seemed kind and her touch was gentle, but she forced a vile-tasting potion down Tori's throat that made her violently sick. Another block of time—Tori could not have said if it was hours or minutes—passed in a blur. The next thing she knew, the man—the doctor, she suspected—was hovering over her, some sort of scalpel in his hand. He took hold of her arm and drew it straight.

"No," Tori said and tried to pull it free. Fear rose in her chest, but her arm seemed to weigh a ton. She tossed on the bed.

"May, come hold her," the doctor said and the woman, who Tori had not realized was present, took hold of Tori's wrist and held it securely. She placed her other hand on Tori's shoulder, effectively immobilizing her.

"No," Tori protested again.

"Hush, it is all right. We are only trying to help you," the woman, May, said.

Tori screamed when the doctor sliced her arm at the inner elbow. It wasn't until he placed a bowl under her wound to collect the blood that she realized they were bleeding her. She had forgotten how primitive medicine was in the nineteenth century. She stopped fighting, realizing it was pointless anyway, and hoped they wouldn't take too much blood, weakening her further. Her head spun and she felt nauseated when the doctor finally tied a scrap of fabric around her arm. She hoped it was clean.

"Sebastien," she murmured.

"The young man who brought you in? He has returned to his boat," May said.

"Is he gone?" Tears pricked at the back of her eyes. Had he abandoned her to this strange world? Of course, he had no reason to help her, no responsibility for her. But his was the first face she'd seen upon jumping to this time, and he gave her a sense of security. She felt so lost at the mercy of nineteenth-century medicine. Her current helplessness, coupled with a sense of doom she couldn't shake, made her want to scream.

"I don't know. The keelers are a wild bunch and don't tend to stay in town for long."

Tori tried to choke down her panic. She was feeling a bit better, and tried to recall what Sebastien and the priest had said before her collapse. Father Andre had offered to find her a place to stay until Sebastien came back up the river. She had no idea how long that would take, but guessed it would be months. She would be an unwanted burden on the family and would be expected to earn her keep in a time when she didn't know how to do anything. She grabbed at May's arm, dismayed by how weak she still felt. "Can you get a message to him if he's still here? I want to go with him."

"I could send the housemaid down to the river, I suppose. He might be willing to come see you, but I don't know about taking you on as a passenger. It's my understanding you have no money to pay for passage."

"I have no money for room and board either. Maybe we could work something out. I could cook for the men..." Tori's voice trailed off. Her microwave skills would do little to help her here, and even her ability to whip something up on the stove top depended on convenience products. She had been camping a time or two, but her experience at cooking over an open flame was pretty much limited to roasting hot dogs and marshmallows.

"It just wouldn't be proper, my dear, you alone with all those men. The settlers come down on the boats, but they are with their families. A keelboat is no place for a woman, especially one who is already ill."

"But you will send the message?"

May nodded, although she looked troubled.

"Thank you." Tori sank back onto her pillow, allowing exhaustion to overwhelm her. May left the room, presumably to send the servant girl on her errand. As soon as she was alone, doubts began to prickle at her consciousness. May's words rang in her mind. She would be the only woman among a group of rowdy men. She didn't really know Sebastien at all, even though he made her feel safe. She thought she had known Ned, at least a little bit, and look how that had turned out. Perhaps it would be better to throw herself at the mercy of a charitable family. She curled into a ball as sleep overtook her. If only she could go home...

* * *

Tori wasn't sure how long she slept, but when she awoke, Sebastien sat by her bedside. He was writing in a journal of some sort, but when he saw she was awake, he put the book aside.

"Doctor Bennett says you are improving, Miss Foster."

Tori pushed herself up to a sitting position, experiencing only mild dizziness. She agreed with the doctor's assessment, but thought her recovery was in spite of the doctor's treatment, not because of it. "I feel better."

"I understand you wanted to see me." He reached for her hand and squeezed it gently. "I can't take you aboard, Victoria. I don't take on passengers. But Father Andre will find you someplace to stay."

"Why don't you take passengers?"

He grinned. "Too much trouble for too little reward. Barrels of goods don't require feeding and don't complain."

"I won't complain," Tori said, but wondered if that was a promise she could keep. Life on a nineteenth-century keelboat would be rough, rougher than staying ashore.

"We will be leaving tomorrow or the next day, and you're still ill."

"But getting better."

"Why do you want to come with us? Have you recovered more of your memories?"

Why did she feel so strongly about returning to the river? Was it merely the level of competence Sebastien radiated that made her feel safe, or was it the pull of the Mississippi itself? She had been near the river when she'd been pulled back in time, and she instinctively felt she needed to be near it again if she had any hope of returning to her own century. There was also the locket, of course. She remembered how it had glowed and pulsed. She felt sure the locket was the key, though she thought the river had played a part. "If I fell from a boat, that boat has probably continued to float downstream. My best chance of finding out where I belong is to continue down river."

Sebastien appeared to consider her words. "Boats put in here every day. If you really want passage downstream, you could find it somewhere else."

"I don't have any money."

Sebastien's steel-blue eyes seemed chillier and less warm. "Then why would I want to take you?"

Good question. "You saved me. Please don't abandon me now." *Obviously the old Chinese belief of being responsible for the life you saved hasn't made it to frontier America yet.* His eyes were growing more distant by the minute. She scrambled for another way to persuade him. "I might have money, if I find the boat I was on. I must have paid for passage."

"I am sorry, but you will be better off here."

She had one thing of value, something she was unwilling to give up, but Sebastien didn't have to know that. She pulled the necklace from beneath her borrowed shirt. "I have this. I could give it to you after we reach our destination if it turns out I have no money to pay you."

"The necklace for passage to New Orleans?"

Tori hesitated. She wasn't sure how she had activated the necklace in the first place. If she failed to return home, she didn't want to be stuck in New Orleans. "To St. Louis. If I don't find the boat I fell from on the way downriver, then I want to come back up." At least then she would be home, even though St. Louis in 1811 was probably anything like the sprawling metropolis she knew.

"May I see it?"

Tori reluctantly lifted it free of her neck and handed it over. She watched Sebastien run his strong fingers over the stone. He wasn't a particularly tall or bulky, but his strength was evident in nearly every move he made. "It's beautiful. Very unusual. Probably worth a considerable sum, but I'm no expert."

"Then you'll do it?" Tori felt nervous every second the necklace was out of her possession, but the thought of staying in Ste. Genevieve filled her with fear.

He appeared tempted, but then a shadow crossed his face. "No. I'm sorry, but my ban on passengers still holds." He returned the necklace.

She slipped it back over her head, tucking it carefully beneath her shirt. "I see." Panic nibbled at the edge of her mind, but she tried to be reasonable. She had left the twenty-first century from Ste. Gen. Maybe staying here was her best chance of finding her way home.

"I will honor the promise I made to Father Andre. If you are still here by the time I return, I will take you to St. Louis. If no other opportunities present themselves, my stepmother can take you on as a servant."

Great. Months of living as an unpaid drudge in Ste. Genevieve and then living the rest of my life as a servant in nineteenth-century St. Louis? She *had* to find a way home. She supposed she should feel grateful that they weren't just throwing her out into the winter cold to freeze and starve to death, but it was difficult to dredge up any gratitude in her current situation, which continued to go from bad to worse.

"I'm glad to see you doing so much better. I wish you well, truly." He stood, preparing to leave.

Something tugged at Tori's memory, a vague worry that had swirled beneath all her other problems, only now reaching up to the surface. "Be careful, Sebastien. There's danger on the river."

He smiled down at her. "There is always danger on the Mississippi. You're proof of that."

"No, I mean something else. Something coming."

The smile faded from his eyes, although it never left his lips. "I've always been a survivor, Miss Foster. I don't intend to quit now."

Chapter 9

Exhausted by her failed bargaining session with Sebastien, Tori slipped back into sleep. She awakened when May came in with a tray of bread and broth. The food, meager as it was, smelled wonderful and Tori realized her appetite had returned twofold. She dipped a chunk of bread into the broth. The bread tore easily and was still warm from the oven. Tori had to force herself to eat slowly.

"I'm sorry you were unable to persuade Mr. La Roche to take you on board, but you'll be pleased to know that Father Andre has found a family willing to take you in. They have several children already and the wife is expecting another. She could use the help."

Tori cringed. She liked children well enough, but had little experience with them other than Anne's daughter, and Hannah always seemed better behaved than most of the kids Tori saw dragged around by their exhausted mothers. She never accepted any students younger than seven and even then—well, it seemed she hadn't the requisite patience. "I'm sure that will do nicely," she forced herself to say, since May looked so happy for her.

"We'll get you moved over there as soon as Dr. Bennett says you're well enough."

Tori finished the simple meal. "Thank you, that was delicious," she said. She meant it, but wished she could follow up with a hamburger and fries. Unfortunately McDonald's wouldn't be invented for a another one hundred fifty years.

May gathered up the dishes and left. Tori lay back down and nearly let sleep take her away again. She was still very tired and the mere act of eating had drained her reserves. But when she closed her eyes, she remembered visiting the general store with Sebastien. He had not been the only one trading with the proprietor. The owner of the other keelboat had also been present. Perhaps he would be amenable to taking passengers.

Tori didn't think they had been introduced; even if they had, she didn't remember his name. A summons from a servant girl was unlikely to bring him to her sickbed, even if May would be willing to send the girl again. She would have to approach him herself, and soon, before the boats left town.

Tori hauled herself out of bed. Her head swam and her muscles protested, but she persisted. To her surprise, she found her clothing hanging in the closet. Her boots were still damp, but no longer soaking. Even her coat was mostly dry.

Not wanting to alert May to her actions, she crept from the room after glancing down the hallway in both directions. There was no sign of the doctor, May, or any servants. She heard voices from the rear of the house and took care not to make any noise as she moved in the opposite direction. She had a vague memory of Sebastien placing her on the table in the exam room and she shuddered as she passed it. Thank goodness she had not been seriously ill or injured. She would have to take great care to stay healthy until she could return to her own time and the miracle of modern medicine.

What if I'm unable to go back? Tori refused to give the misgiving much credence. *I have to find my way back. That's all there is to it.*

Unsure of which way to go when she stepped from the house, Tori headed downhill. She knew she would find the river at the lowest point. Sure enough, she soon found herself on Main Street, near where the boats were tied up. Ignoring the *Fury*, she asked one of the boat men if she could speak to the captain of the other boat.

"You wanna talk to the Rattler?" he asked in surprise. He hawked, spit something to one side and then eyed her again. "Guess there's no harm to it. Get the patron," he called to one of the men on board the keelboat. "Seems the lady wants to talk to him." He drew out the word "lady" until it had three or four syllables and made it sound rather risque.

Tori tamped down her annoyance. If she was to travel with a bunch of rude men, she needed to get used to such treatment. She didn't have to wait long—which was good, since her strength was ebbing away by the minute. The man sprang over the side of his boat with the same easy grace as Sebastien, but he wasn't quite as well-muscled.

"What can I do for you?" he asked with a cocky grin when he reached the shore.

"I'm the woman Mr. La Roche rescued from the river," Tori began.

He laughed. "I know who you are, Miss Foster. Pulling women from the water isn't an everyday occurrence, even for us river rats. Plus, I don't think I've ever seen anyone else with such a strange looking coat."

Relieved to be back in her own comfortable garments, she hadn't considered how odd they must look to the people of this time. "It is fashionable back East," she said.

His eyes, a lighter blue than Sebastien's, lit with amusement. "Is it? We find it very difficult to keep up with fashions here in the West."

Tori got the distinct impression that he didn't believe her claim for a minute. "You have the advantage of me. You know my name, but I'm unsure what to call you. Would that be Mr. Rattler?"

He laughed again, harder than before. "You can call me that if you like. Or you can call me Bob or Mr. Rivers. I'll answer to them all. Heck, most of the men just call me Rat. Behind my back, of course."

"Of course." She hurried on before she lost her nerve. She found herself wondering what would have happened to her if it had been Rat who'd found her instead of Sebastien. "I would like to book passage on your boat."

He cocked his head to one side. "Thought you didn't have any money."

"I hoped we could reach an agreement. Obviously I can't paddle, but perhaps I could do the cooking."

"We've already got a cook."

Tori fingered the necklace under her shirt. She didn't want to offer it to Rat/Bob. She stared out at the river, watching it flow past. She could feel its pull. Gritting her teeth, she lifted the pendant from its hiding place. "I have this," she said. "Take me to New Orleans and it's yours," she lied, once again.

"Let me see." He held out his hand.

She let him touch and examine it, but didn't take it from her neck.

"Give it to me now and I'll let you on board."

"No. When we reach our destination."

"What's going on here?"

Tori recognized Sebastien's voice immediately, but she was surprised that he'd managed to sneak up behind her. "I'm offering Mr. Rivers the same choice I gave you earlier."

"Put that away. Do you know nothing of the character of the men who work these boats? Any one of them might slit your throat for that bauble."

"Stabbed through the heart," Bob said and placed a hand over his chest. "Whatever will the young lady think of me?"

"No need to deal with the Rattler. I accept your offer," Sebastien said shortly.

"Really? That's great." And a major relief. Bob had given her a bad vibe.

"You can have my cabin. I'll bunk with Roger."

"Thank you." She felt bad for kicking him out of his quarters, but not bad enough to change her mind. If she was lucky, she would be gone within the next few days and Sebastien could move back in. Without the necklace, of course, but also without her oh-so-troublesome presence.

"We leave at first light tomorrow, so you might as well enjoy one last night of comfort before coming on board."

Tori nodded, then realized for the first time that she had no money to pay the doctor's fee. "Do you think Dr. Bennett will be willing to wait until our return to get paid?" Tori had no intention of still being in this century when the *Fury* docked once more at Ste. Genevieve, so she would be stiffing the doctor as well. *Oh well, it can't be helped.* Besides, although Tori felt she owed him for room and board for a few days, she also thought he should pay *her* for the barbaric treatment he'd subjected her to.

He had been watching her, a small smile on his lips. "I already paid him."

Tori's eyes widened and she studied Sebastien's rugged features. Bushy eyebrows shaded the intensity of his blue eyes and a scruffy beard softened his square jawline. "Truly? That was very kind of you."

"Thought it was the least I could do, seeing as how I pulled you from the river."

Like taking an injured animal to the vet. Tori was nonetheless grateful and felt all the more confident that she had made the right decision. "I'll see you in the morning."

Sebastien nodded and she began to retrace her steps back to the doctor's office. She wondered if she had been missed yet, and if so, where they thought she had gone. She turned to glance once more at the river. A piece of driftwood swirled past, caught in the torrent. Sebastien was talking to Bob, a thunderous expression on his face. Tori suppressed a smile of victory and continued on her way.

* * *

She had forced his hand. Sebastien took his frustration out on the Rattler. "You knew I didn't want her aboard." They still stood on the river's bank, the bustle of goods being loaded and unloaded from their boats proceeding around them.

"Then why did you take her?"

"Because you were going to."

"How do you know?"

"Maybe you wanted the necklace, maybe you just wanted to annoy me. Hell, I don't know why, but I'm damn sure you were going to accept her request."

"I was considering it," Rivers admitted with a grin. "So why not let me accept the risk and hassle? I don't think she intends to part with her jewels."

"What makes you say that?"

"She didn't even want me to touch it and she refused to pay in advance."

She let me hold it. Sebastien kept that information to himself. "Smart of her. We could take the necklace and abandon her along the way."

"True, but I consider myself a straight shooter."

Sebastien raised an eyebrow. "You're named after a rattlesnake."

"I didn't choose my nickname."

No, but you probably earned it. "I trust her."

"You're allowing yourself to be fooled by a pretty face."

"Don't be ridiculous. My offer has nothing to do with her looks." *Or does it?* He longed to touch her pale hair and fair, soft skin. "I didn't save her from the river only to let her be violated or murdered by one of your crew."

Rivers laughed. "Because your men are all choir boys."

Sebastien smiled. He couldn't help it. Rivers might rub him the wrong way, but he oozed charisma. If he continued with the keel boat trade he might end up as famous as Mike Fink, the legendary keelboat operator about whom dozens of tall tales were told. "I'll keep an eye on my men."

"I don't envy you the task."

Sebastien grunted in agreement. "She is stubborn." He couldn't help but admire her for her grit. She had gotten him to take her aboard even when he was dead set against it.

"And deceitful. Don't forget that. That ugly coat of hers is no more fashionable on the East Coast than out here."

Sebastien's gut tightened. For all that he was drawn to her beauty, a rare commodity on the frontier, part of him knew that Rivers spoke the truth about this, at least. Sebastien wouldn't risk turning his back on his quasi-partner, but there was something the enigmatic Miss Foster was keeping to herself. "Well, that's my problem."

"I'm surprised you paid her medical bills."

"Father Andre persuaded me it was my duty as a Christian."

"Word on the river is that you're more motivated by profit than piousness."

Sebastien scowled. He knew he drove a tough bargain, but thought himself fair in his dealings. "I'm a riverman, not a priest. I won't allow myself to be cheated."

"So I've heard." Rivers squinted his eyes and gazed downriver. "It's a long way to New Orleans. Reckon I'll go scare up a good meal."

Sebastien watched him go. There was definitely something snake-like about the man. He went to find Roger. "Seems we will be taking Miss Foster along with us," he told the older man. "She'll take my cabin and I'll share yours."

"Some of the men won't be happy."

"I know, but superstitions about women aboard ship are silly. Just think how many settlers have come into the territory in the last few years."

"Things didn't end well with your sister."

Sebastien had to take a deep breath before he could respond. "Miss Foster is not my sister. She seems to have recovered from her illness and is determined to head toward New Orleans. We might as well reap the reward. If the men give you any trouble, tell them to find another boat. I won't stand for any insolence."

Roger nodded, but didn't look happy.

"What?"

"A woman alone might be nothing, but a woman combined with the comet? I just don't like it."

"Not you, too. Roger, you should be old enough by now to know that life's more pain than promise. Now get your butt moving."

"Aye, Captain, but you know as well as I do that something's coming. Something big."

"We need to keep an eye out for Indians. Unrest is growing among the tribes. And we could have trouble with the British soon if those fools in Washington declare war. I realize that times are changing and maybe that comet is a harbinger of bad luck. But more likely it's just some big ol' rock floating through the sky."

"What would your mother have thought?" Roger asked, before heading up the gangplank.

She would have taken it as an omen. Sebastien turned to bark an order at the nearest member of his crew. Comet or no comet, they needed to be ready to leave by dawn.

Chapter 10

Tori arrived at the *Fury* well before dawn. She wouldn't put it past Sebastien to sail without her if she gave him the slightest opportunity. Some of the men gave her surly looks as she climbed on board, but she did her best to ignore them. She was starting out on an adventure and her spirits were high. She even carried a small valise.

Upon learning of her plans, May had tried to talk her out of traveling to New Orleans, but when Tori remained obstinate, May had taken her back to the church and ordered Father Andre to raid the poor box. They found a couple of worn but wearable dresses and undergarments that had been donated to the church for the poor, as well as the luggage. Tori had hoped to find some shoes so she wouldn't always have to wear her Uggs, but her feet were too big for any of the cast offs. May obviously thought Tori's feet were on the large size, which amused Tori—in modern times her feet were average at most—but she kept this tidbit to herself. As a last resort, they had checked the men's bin and found a ratty pair of slippers.

"They'll have to do," Tori said. The soles were nearly worn through, but they were soft and comfortable.

"Are you sure you're doing the right thing? If you don't fancy being a nursemaid, perhaps Dr. Bennett could take you on and train you to be a nurse, like he's training me."

Tori had grown fond of May in the small time she had known her, but the thought of being trained in nineteenth-century medicine horrified her. "I don't really have any interest in medicine, but you're doing an excellent job."

"I like helping people, but that's not why I'm training with Dr. Bennett. If it comes to war, nurses will be in demand and I'll be able to earn a nice dowry. I want to marry some day and my family doesn't have much money."

"War?" A shiver of trepidation tore down Tori's spine. "What war?"

May gazed at her wide-eyed. "I keep forgetting you've lost most of your memory. I was talking about war with England, although even the Indian troubles are increasing."

Tori could have smacked herself. Sebastien had told her it was 1811; soon America would be embroiled in the War of 1812. She wished she could remember exactly when the conflict started. "I expect you're right," she said carefully. "Will you go East, to nurse soldiers, if we do go to war?"

"I expect we'll have our share of wounded right here. There'd be no need to go East."

Not a comforting thought. Somehow Tori had always pictured the War of 1812 being fought on the East Coast and at sea. Had there been battles in the West? She couldn't remember and wished she'd paid more attention in history class. She did recall the Battle of New Orleans, but it had been fought near the end of the war. Well, technically it had been fought *after* the war, since the peace treaty had been signed a few months prior to the skirmish. One way or the other, she would be long gone from New Orleans before then. At least she hoped she would be. In the meantime, she needed to do her best to blend in. Until she figured out a way to get home, she was vulnerable.

Tori placed her valise in Sebastien's cabin and wandered back on deck. The men on both the *Fury* and Bob Rivers' boat, the *Revenge*, were busy getting ready to shove off. As they drifted away from the bank, Tori was touched to see that May had come to see her off. She wouldn't be due at Dr. Bennett's yet for hours, so she had gotten up early for Tori's benefit. She stood on the shore, bundled against the cold, and waved. Tori waved back.

"You seem to have made a friend."

She glanced over at Sebastien. He had not made much noise, but she had been aware of his magnetic presence behind her. "She was very kind to me." *Well, except when she was holding me down so Dr. Bennett could draw blood from me like a vampire.*

Our next stop will be New Madrid. After that, there are only small settlements until Natchez."

Tori froze, wishing Anne were here so she could ask her some questions. "New Madrid?" she managed.

"A sizable community just south of where the Ohio flows into the Mississippi."

The niggling fear she had felt for the last several days—ever since coming to accept that she really had traveled through time—coalesced in her belly. After her discussion with May yesterday, she had thought maybe it was the War of 1812 that seemed to hang over her head like an ax. But it wasn't the war at all. It was the earthquakes.

Perhaps her memory had been affected by the time jump. Not only were her last memories of her own time rather fuzzy, but she had only now realized she was about to have a front-row seat to one of the most massive earthquakes to ever strike the United States. It hadn't been the deadliest, not by a long shot, but that was probably only because population in the area was sparse. She tried to recall everything Anne had ever told her about the quakes. Her friend had been rather obsessed with them, even though they had not caused nearly as much damage in Ste. Gen as they had in New Madrid, western Tennessee, and northeastern Arkansas. Experts argued, but local legends insisted that during at least one of the quakes, the Mississippi had run backward. The same river she was now traversing in a relatively small boat made of nothing sturdier than wood. The quake had produced waterfalls, sand blows and fissures in the ground. Whole towns had been destroyed. Reelfoot Lake, a state park in Tennessee, had been created, destroying a Native American village.

Although she couldn't remember the exact dates, she knew there had been a series of quakes starting in 1811 and continuing through early 1812. There had been thousands of quakes in total, but three had been huge, estimated in her time at over eight on the Richter scale. It was already December. The earthquake could hit at any time. People had died on the river. She wasn't sure how many, didn't think anyone knew, but realized she would have been safer staying in Ste. Genevieve. Safer, but further away from her goal of getting home. She felt sure of this, though there was no way to prove her theory.

"We shouldn't be on the river. It isn't safe."

Sebastien gave her a strange look. "I tried to convince you not to come. You insisted."

She realized she must appear crazy to him. She almost felt as if she was. "Yes, of course—I'm not telling you anything you don't already know." *But you don't know an earthquake is coming!* She searched for a reason to explain her erratic behavior without telling the truth—which he would never believe. "I think I'm starting to recall how I fell from the boat and nearly drowned."

His gaze sharpened. "What do you remember?"

"No details. Just the feeling, the overwhelming terror of water closing over my head." *Lying's getting easier.* Actually, on some level she didn't think she was lying. Suddenly she could remember the shock of cold, the struggle to swim trussed up in her coat and weighted down by her boots. The snow falling like a heavy, bone-chilling shroud, and the eerie light show in the sky. She recalled the warmth of the necklace, how it had thrummed in time to the thunder and glowed along with the lightning. And finally darkness. She shivered.

"Are you warm enough?"

Tori smiled. "Yes, this coat is…" *Rated for below freezing.* "Um, very warm."

Sebastien reached over and touched the fabric. "It's soft, but unusual. It's not fur or wool. What is the material?"

Something new age, Tori guessed, but she couldn't say that. "I'm not sure. It's imported from Europe."

"It's difficult to get foreign goods with the war between Britain and France and the embargo set by Congress."

"Some things get through."

"And coats such as these are all the rage in Philadelphia?"

Tori shrugged. "I may have exaggerated a bit. They are desirable, but difficult to find, as you said. I was lucky to get my hands on one." She supposed she should be grateful she had been wearing her concert costume when she made her impromptu trip to the past. Otherwise she would probably have shocked everyone by wearing pants. She had the impression that Sebastien wanted to ask her more questions, but he refrained.

"Would you like to come up top with me? You'll have a good view of the river."

"Sure." Tori didn't know what he meant by 'up top.' There was no second deck on the boat. She allowed him to take her hand and haul her up onto the cabin roof.

"This is where I spend most of my time, especially when we're going down stream. Drifting with the current is easy, but the speed makes it more dangerous. Hauling this beauty against the current takes sweat and effort, but the going is slow enough to spot most hazards before they bite you in the... derriere."

Tori nearly giggled. Like she hadn't heard the word "ass" before. "Your men curse freely in front of me."

"I have aspirations to being a gentleman. That's why I also brought this." He waved a blanket at her before folding it up in a square and placing it on the cabin roof. Tori sank down on it, grateful for both the padding and the warmth. Sebastien took his place beside her and began directing his men.

Tori sat and watched the river for a while. It was peaceful floating in the brisk morning air. Everything here seemed crystal clear as if her old life had been viewed through a foggy lens. *Was there really so much pollution back home?* They saw other boats, more than she would have expected. They passed several lumbering flatboats, and Tori marveled at the variety of goods, especially live animals, they often carried. When she asked about the boats filled with people and animals, rather than boxes of cargo, Sebastien explained to her that pioneers moving west often transported all their possessions, livestock and families aboard the crafts.

"Looks kind of risky," Tori said, comparing the box-shaped boats to the sleek lines of the *Fury*. "How often do they sink?"

"It depends how well they are built. Most will be fine unless they strike debris or encounter turbulent conditions."

"You're not using them."

"I started with flatboats. They're cheap, but they can't come back up the river. When they reach their destination, they will be sold for scrap or cut up for firewood. Once I had saved enough money, I invested in the *Fury*." Sebastien seemed to enjoy answering her questions, but didn't talk much otherwise. He kept a wary eye on the river, calling instructions to his crew whenever he spotted an obstacle.

In addition to the watercraft, animals also seemed abundant. Birds flew overhead and she could hear them twittering from shore. The first time she saw a deer come up to drink, she exclaimed in delight.

Sebastien gave her one of his funny looks. "You act like you've never seen deer before."

"Of course, I've seen deer. I just think they're pretty."

"Pretty? More like tasty. I may send a hunting party ashore later."

She swallowed. *Guess there's no going to the supermarket and buying a package of meat wrapped in plastic.* She couldn't lose sight of where and *when* she was. "Do you catch many deer?"

"We bring down one or two per trip. Fresh meat makes a pleasant change from corn, potatoes, and hardtack."

Tori didn't know what hardtack was, but suspected she would find out before too long. "What about fish?"

"We'll cast a line here or there."

Tori thought the water must be teeming with fish if the wildlife on shore was any indication. In addition to the deer, she soon spotted foxes, squirrels, and raccoons. But the land seemed almost barren of human habitation. The occasional farm dotted the landscape, but mostly she viewed an endless vista of trees. When she tired of the view, she turned her attention to Sebastien. He remained focused on the water, calling directions out to his crew.

"What are you looking for? Indians?" A chill snaked down her spine.

"We all keep on the look-out for Indians and pirates, but it's my job to steer clear of the planters and sawyers."

Planters and sawyers? The first made her think of plantation owners, and the second of Mark Twain's classic novel, *Tom Sawyer*. She started to say something about it, snatching back her words when she realized the famous book had not yet been written. "What are those?" she asked instead.

"Trees fall into the river all the time. A planter is a tree where one end gets stuck in the bottom and the other end is floating beneath the surface ready to tear a hole in the bottom of a boat. Sawyers are similar, but easier to spot since their free end bobs up and down in the water. Most boatmen with a few voyages under their belt can see the sawyers coming, but it takes a good eye to spot planters."

"So that's how you got your nickname."

Sebastien nodded.

"How did Mr. Rivers get his?"

"No idea. Bob and I haven't known each other long. Started hearing tales about his exploits a few years ago, so when he offered to partner with me on this venture, I agreed."

"You don't trust him."

"Never heard nothing bad about him, but boatmen as a whole have a rough reputation. Pirates ply their trade on the Mississippi and it can be hard to tell the difference between an honest trader and a thief."

"Where do you fall on that spectrum?"

His lip twisted up in a half smirk. "I'm no pirate."

"Why do you do it if you have to face Indians, pirates, planters and sawyers? And that's before you make the long journey home."

"You forgot to mention islands, sandbars, and storms. Run aground and the patron can lose hours or even days. Sometimes an entire cargo is lost."

"Is it worth it?"

"Yes. You can make a tidy profit once you reach New Orleans."

"Is this what you've always done? Did you start out as one of the crew?"

"No. My father was a trapper, and at first I followed in his footsteps. Eventually I convinced him to take a flatboat downriver with our furs. Things evolved from there." Some of the playfulness bled away from his expression, leaving him looking more like the Sebastien she was beginning to know.

"So you no longer do any trapping?"

"Some, but game grows scarcer with every passing year. You have to go all the way to Colorado now to find enough beaver to make a living."

Tori was shocked. She glanced over at the passing bank, which still appeared a veritable wilderness to her, and felt a pang of sadness as she realized how much worse things had become in her own time.

Sebastien jumped down from the roof. "Man the roof, Roger. I'm going to take a handful of men ashore and see if we can bag us some dinner."

"Aye, captain," the older man said and hopped spryly up next to Tori. "Keep watch on shore, young lady. I'll look for river hazards, but if you see any of the human variety, let me know and we'll sound the horn and bring in the boys."

Tori nodded, although she had her doubts about her ability to spot Indians or pirates hiding in the woods. She had never been good and hide and seek.

Chapter 11

Tori sat with Roger for a couple more hours, then pleaded fatigue. Still not fully recovered from her illness, she went down to the cabin and crawled into the bunk. Uncomfortable as it was, she fell asleep almost instantly. Dreams of fire and lightning and heaving earth filled her mind and she woke with her heart pounding.

The sound came again. *Was it the earthquake?* No, someone was knocking on the cabin door. "Come in."

Roger stuck his head in the room. "The hunters aren't back yet, but the rest of us are having a bite to eat. Thought you might want to join us."

"Thank you." Tori sat up as he closed the door behind him. It wasn't much warmer in the cabin than it was outside, so she hadn't undressed, only removed her coat. She put it back on and went out on deck. Roger handed her a handful of crackers and an apple taken from a barrel. The men who had stayed on board were already half done. Tori bit into one of the crackers. It looked dry and tasteless and felt like sawdust in her mouth. "Hardtack?"

"Yes. Guess you don't eat that much back East," Roger said.

"No, this is my first time."

"You'll get used to it," one of the men said. "Just don't break your teeth on it."

"Good advice." She finished her first piece and forced another one down. She was hungry and didn't know when she would be able to eat again. Reaching her limit at three, Tori set the rest aside and started on the apple. It didn't taste quite as she expected, but it was sweet and refreshing after the bland biscuit.

After lunch, the men took off. A few wielded paddles, some cleaned the already tidy deck and the others lounged around. Going down river was easy; coming back up would require every ounce of stamina they had.

Tori wandered toward the stern. She glanced around to make sure no one was watching and then pulled the necklace from beneath her shirt. The deep blue stone lay innocently in its silver frame. It didn't glow, pulse, or hum. It felt cool to the touch. How had she activated it back in the twenty-first century and could she duplicate the process now?

She stood there for a long time, but nothing happened. The stone mocked her, refusing to come to life. Finally, she gave up, slumping against the side of the boat. Nothing. She didn't know how to work the stone and might be trapped here forever.

She pushed herself up and returned to the cabin. A bookcase with a small desk area beneath it stood against one wall. She rifled through the desk until she found some paper and a quill pen. A jar of ink sat on top of the desk. Tori had never written with a quill pen, but she dipped it in the ink and tried to write on the paper. The pen scratched across the paper, making a thin wobbly line, and the ink only lasted long enough for her to write a couple of words. She kept at it and eventually made a list of everything she could remember about that fateful night when she'd traveled more than two hundred years into the past.

It had been cold and snowing. Thunder and lightning lit the sky. The concert ended at ten, so it had been somewhere between ten and eleven at night. She'd argued with the obnoxious Mr. Henderson, father to her reluctant student Jason. Although she had exaggerated her loss of memory to Sebastien and the others to avoid difficult questions, her last moments in the twenty-first century were a bit hazy. Had Mr. Henderson run her off the road with his car? It seemed unlikely. Character assassination seemed more his style. Why risk an attempted murder charge when he could just get her fired? Again.

The car had startled her. She must have slipped. The ground had been covered with snow, and it had continued to fall fast and heavy. Her vision had been obscured, her footing treacherous. But another possibility lurked in the back of her mind, one she didn't want to examine too closely. She clearly recalled how the river had called to her: slow, languorous, deep... welcoming. She'd lost her job and her home, had been attacked by a man she had considered a friend and threatened by one she knew disliked her. She still missed her mother and, were it not for Anne, would consider herself alone in the world. Had she jumped? Had circumstances overwhelmed her to the point where she had tried to take her own life? She didn't think she was suicidal and had made no plans to end her life, but might she have acted on impulse?

Tori wasn't sure, but she guessed it had nothing to do with the problem at hand—how to return to her own time. Three things stood out for her: the lightning, her heightened emotions, and the river. She suspected she needed at least one and perhaps all three to align to activate the stone. Just now, she'd had only one or perhaps two of the three. She'd been near the river and determined to return to her own time, but there had been no lightning. And determination might not be a strong enough emotion.

She folded the piece of paper and placed it in her pocket. She needed to be ready the next time it stormed. However, since it was December, that might not be for many months. She might be trapped here for the duration of the earthquakes.

She didn't want to consider that she might never return home.

***

It wasn't as bad having a woman on board as Sebastien had expected. Victoria didn't prattle incessantly, as many of the young women he knew did, and he thought she made a genuine effort to fit in and be as little trouble as possible. Nevertheless, he suspected her life back East was very different than her current experiences. She didn't complain, but she'd lost weight and gone pale with fatigue in spite of the fact that she was required to do very little physical labor. She couldn't seem to adjust to the constant cold and their poor diet didn't seem to agree with her.

He enjoyed her company when they both sat on the cabin roof. He'd taught her a bit about navigation; she could now spot most sawyers they came across, and had even noticed a planter. She'd memorized the various islands included in *The Navigator*, a book printed every few years to help captains negotiate the treacherous waters of the Mississippi and Ohio. She'd also learned the names of everyone on his crew, and the men appeared willing to accept her.

Sebastien expected to reach New Madrid by nightfall. They would stop longer there, taking on some supplies and trade goods as well as selling some of what they had taken on in St. Louis to the New Madrid merchants. New Madrid was built on a bend in the river, and like all bends, it provided unique challenges to river traffic. Eddies were often unpredictable, and erosion of the river bank created sandbars and sometimes temporary "islands" of intertwined trees and dirt. Still, it was a busy port with often dozens of boats at rest, and the mood of the hands was jovial as they anticipated a few days of carousing and mischief.

Sebastien shared some of their enthusiasm, but as he was the patron and responsible for the *Fury* and her cargo, he had less time for leisure. Victoria would probably appreciate a chance to stand on dry land and savor some good cooking. If they happened to be in port on a Sunday, he would invite her to the weekly dance.

As the shadows lengthened and afternoon drew on, one of the men brought out a fiddle and began scratching out a tune. Some of the men sang along and a few got up and danced. Sebastien caught

Victoria eying the fiddler, her bow-shaped mouth pursed in disapproval.

"You don't like music? I've not much use for it myself, but the men enjoy it and it helps pass the time."

"I love music! I lost my violin in the river, remember? I'm just not sure I'd call the noise he's making 'music.'"

"Some patrons hire a fiddler special, but I think it a waste of money. Dalton's a good keeler and he plays the fiddle. So, while he may not be the best, he's all we've got."

"You've got me, but I no longer have my violin."

"Maybe it's still aboard the boat you fell from."

"Maybe." She frowned.

"So you play better than Dalton?"

Victoria just rolled her eyes.

"Dalton, let the lady have a go."

Dalton, a scrawny young man with wiry muscles, seemed to take her measure. "I don't let just anyone touch my fiddle."

"I'll take good care of it," she said with a smile.

Dalton ran the bow one more time down the strings. "Okay." He handed her the instrument, a look of challenge on his face.

Victoria accepted it as if he had handed her his first born baby. She ran gentle fingers down the casing and then cradled it against her chin. "Let me show you how it's done, boys."

Sebastien caught the flash of anger in Dalton's eyes, but Victoria already seemed lost in a daze. He hoped he wouldn't regret his impulse.

She ran the bow down the strings. It didn't sound all that different to him than when Dalton did it, but then he'd never had an ear for music. When a few of the men jeered, however, he thought they might agree with him.

Victoria appeared unfazed. "Any requests?"

No one spoke for a moment, then a man asked for Bach. There were boos and hisses as well as a few hoots of approval.

"Very well." She closed her eyes and appeared to think. Then she glided the bow across the strings and a haunting melody poured from the instrument. The men fell quiet after a few minutes. Even Dalton's jaw dropped. She played for several minutes and when she played the final notes, one of the men began clapping. The others followed suit—everyone, except Dalton, who glared at her from where he sulked at the edge of the group.

"You're a talented musician, Victoria. Was that why you were on the river? Were you with a troop of traveling performers?" Sebastien asked.

Victoria's eyes grew wide. "I think you figured it out. One of my first thoughts was for my violin. I should have realized I was a professional."

"Professional?" Sebastien wasn't familiar with the word.

"Someone who does something as their profession—their occupation."

Sebastien's eyes narrowed, although he didn't allow his smile to slip. She spoke strangely at times, but that might be because she was from the East. Music could explain why a gently-bred young woman was traveling in the wilderness, but she had accepted it too readily. Much as he wanted to, he didn't really believe her. Victoria was hiding something, he just didn't know what. He didn't think she had staged her accident; it was too dangerous. She had nearly drowned and was lucky she hadn't grown even more ill than she had from exposure. But he sometimes suspected that someone had tried to harm her.

But why? She was only a woman. Could she be a British spy? She had no British accent, but he supposed a talented spy wouldn't. Her speech was strange, she used unusual expressions, and sometimes seemed ignorant of even the most basic knowledge. Instinct told him he couldn't trust her, but he also couldn't bring himself to think of her as a spy. He would stay close to her and eventually she would make a mistake.

* * *

Tori was amazed by the bustle of the port when they drew into New Madrid. There must have been at least twenty boats lined up on the shore. The majority of these vessels had come not from St. Louis or farther up the Mississippi, but from the Ohio. She heard both French and English spoken as workers and passengers greeted one another. Old friendships were revived with much back-slapping, and new acquaintances were acquired.

Tori gazed out at the town, marching away from the river in a grid. Like the historical homes in Ste. Genevieve, many were built in the Old French style with vertical logs and porches. Her stomach clenched as she realized that within a few months, the entire town would be swallowed by the river.

Sebastien and the Rattler were soon busy talking to their peers and making deals. Boats carried goods of all kinds, from furniture, farming implements, and other manufactured goods from the East, to whiskey, hemp, and tobacco from Kentucky. Cows, horses, pigs, and dogs created a racket. Barrels of apples, potatoes, and dried fruit, bushels of corn, and other foods exchanged hands. Tori hoped Sebastien would trade some of his cargo for better rations. Although she had grown used to eating hardtack, corn mush, and the occasional treat of wild game, that didn't mean she liked it.

She went ashore with the first wave of men. Roger came with her to secure her a bed and meal in one of the houses that took in paying guests. Sebastien was footing the bill and her guilty conscience nagged at her as a friendly woman showed her to the bed in the attic where she would be sleeping. But there was no way she could give him the necklace. She needed it to return to her own time. At least she had found something useful to do for him. He might not appreciate or see the need for music, but his men enjoyed it and other keelboats employed full-time fiddlers.

"I'm Jenny Sellers," the woman said as she climbed the ladder. "How long will you be in town?"

"I'm not certain." Tori glanced toward Roger.

"A day or two. Depends on how brisk business is."

"Well, tomorrow is Sunday. If you're still here, you should come to the weekly dance."

"Wouldn't miss it," Roger replied.

Tori agreed, but a shiver went down her spine. The first earthquake had struck late Sunday night, or early Monday morning, depending on how you wanted to look at it. Could that be *this* Sunday? Was all hell about to break loose tomorrow? Her heart fluttered as she looked around the home of her hostess. If her memory was correct, most of the buildings in New Madrid had survived the first quake. There had been damage and injuries, but she didn't think there had been any fatalities on the first quake, where the epicenter had been further south. It was the last quake that had spelled doom for the town.

"How long have you lived here?" she asked, thinking the woman wouldn't be living there much longer, at least not in this house. The town would be rebuilt, but never fully recover.

"Five years. We used to live in Kentucky. We heard such good things about it, and while it hasn't quite lived up to it's promise, I like it here."

"Thank you for letting me stay. It's great to be off the boat for awhile."

"You are quite welcome. I enjoy having the company, and the extra income comes in handy."

Her hostess left her alone to freshen up before dinner. Tori eyed the basin of water and towel Jenny had left for her, and longed for a hot shower. She made the best of what she had, however, and was feeling halfway human when she sat down to dinner at the simple plank table.

Jenny introduced Tori to her husband, Eli, and her three children. She brought bowls of vegetables, a roasted chicken, and a loaf of fresh bread to the table. Tori's mouth watered. It seemed a feast after what she'd been having.

She took her time eating, savoring every bite and listening to the conversation around her. Eli farmed a plot of land outside town, but since it was December, he had little to do this time of year except care for the animals and catch up on repairs and maintenance he had let slide during the busy times. The children attended school during the week, but since it was Saturday, the boys had taken a gun into the woods to look for game, while Jenny's daughter had spent the day at a friend's house.

After dinner, they gathered in front of the fire and Eli read from the Bible. Jenny wielded a needle and tackled a large pile of mending. The oldest boy took up a knife and chunk of wood and whittled, but mostly they listened to Eli's deep voice.

Tori almost nodded off a few times during the Bible lesson, and was ready for bed when it was over. The children slept in the attic with her, but her bed was partitioned off by a hanging quilt. There was no fireplace in the attic, but heat rose from downstairs and the snug little house was much warmer than the *Fury*. She undressed and slipped beneath the covers. The mattress, lumpy as it was, still beat Sebastien's narrow cot for comfort. Another quilt, thick and warm and decorated in an intricate pattern, topped her bed. She snuggled beneath it, feeling warm and full for the first time in days. She still worried about the disaster she knew loomed ahead, but exhaustion overtook her and she slipped away.

Chapter 12

Tori awoke the next morning when she heard the children stirring. The boys were arguing.

"I don't want to go back out," the younger said. "We didn't get anything yesterday."

"All the more reason to go out again today," the older said. "I told you to shoot that deer."

"I couldn't. It was just staring at me, and the other animals were too. It was horrible."

"You had a good shot. It didn't look like it was going to move."

"Then why didn't you shoot it?"

"My fingers were numb from the cold."

"So were mine! Besides, that never stopped you before."

Tori, who'd been allowing herself the luxury of wallowing in relative comfort, bolted upright in bed. The argument on the other side of the quilt appeared to devolve into a wrestling match, but she was no longer paying attention. The boys' comments about the animals had triggered a memory. She'd read accounts of strange animal behavior prior to earthquakes. It was as if they had some sort of sixth sense about impending disaster. If that was true in the modern world, it was probably true in 1811 as well. The first quake would strike tonight.

She wanted to warn people, but wasn't sure how to go about it without sounding crazy. She doubted anyone would believe her anyway, and didn't want to end up in a nineteenth-century insane asylum, if such a thing even existed on the frontier. She'd heard horror stories about Bedlam, in England, where the mentally ill had been kept in cages and exhibited to the public for entertainment. She guessed similar institutions existed on the East Coast, but wasn't sure what happened to people out west who were deemed insane. She didn't want to find out. Worse, she might be taken for a witch.

Reluctantly, she threw aside the warmth of the blankets and crawled out into the frigid air. Using the wash basin again, she gave herself a quick sponge bath and pulled on her petticoat, chemise, and a gray wool dress she'd taken from the poor box. The shapeless garment was worn at the elbows and itched wherever it touched her skin, so she tucked a scarf around her neck and into the bodice. At least it was warm, but she added a shawl for extra protection against the cold.

She joined the family for a breakfast of bread toasted over the fire and served with butter or jam and slices of cold ham.

"Would you like some tea?" Jenny asked.

Tori's mood brightened. Though she would have given just about anything for a diet soda, tea sounded so much better than the bitter coffee Roger brewed on the *Fury*. "Yes, please."

"How did you sleep?"

"Wonderful." She curled her hands around the hot mug Jenny gave her and sniffed appreciatively. Jenny sat opposite her with her own cup and Tori watched her chisel a hunk of sugar off a cake and did the same. Bliss.

She soon realized her hosts assumed she would accompany them to church. She made no objection although she wasn't much of a church-goer.

"We attend the Methodist church, but there is a Catholic church in town, if you prefer. We could drop you off on the way."

"I'll come with you," Tori said.

After breakfast they all piled into a wagon pulled by a pair of horses and Eli drove them to a small, plain building. Inside was no fancier. Stark, uncomfortable pews lined the center of the space, and a clear window of bubbly glass let in the light. No stained glass, not that Tori had expected it. It would probably be years before such luxuries reached west of the Mississippi. She had worried that her gown might be too plain, but saw several women dressed no better than she was.

The preacher droned on for a very long time. Quickly losing interest in the man's certainty that they were all destined for hell fire, she had plenty of time to study the congregation. She hoped to see Sebastien, but none of the *Fury*'s crew attended the service. Most of the men and women, like the Sellerses, wore practical garments and were probably shopkeepers and farmers. A few were more richly dressed, and she noted that the ordinary town folk deferred to them. She sighed. Not much had changed in her time. The well-to-do folks made her think of Mr. Henderson and his vendetta against her. If it weren't for him, she didn't think she would be in her current predicament.

When church finally ended, Tori traveled home with the Sellerses for another meal of bread and cold meat, followed by a delicious apple pie. When they finished eating, Eli commandeered the boys to go out to their orchard and help prune the apple trees. Jenny told her daughter, Lizzie, that she could help with the mending or work on a knitting project.

Tori felt odd doing nothing, so she volunteered to help. "I could do some mending. I'm not particularly skilled, but I have sewed before." *In Girl Scouts, years ago.* "I don't know how to knit."

"You don't know how to knit? Didn't your mother teach you?"

"I don't think she knew how either."

Jenny gave her a measuring look. "Do women back East not need to know how to do common household chores? Do servants do it all?"

"We had no servants," Tori said quickly, then wondered how to explain this dichotomy to her hostess. "No live-in servants, but we hired out many of our chores. We had a lady to do our wash, often ate at restaurants, and had a maid come once a week." Satisfied that she had explained the washing machine and dryer as a washerwoman, and the vacuum cleaner as weekly maid service, Tori settled into a chair. "We buy all our clothing ready-made."

"I could teach you, if you'd like to learn," Jenny offered.

"Sure," Tori responded. Knitting had undergone a resurgence in her time and many of her friends knew how, Anne among them. And she needed something to do to pass the time until the dance, when she would see Sebastien again.

Time passed more quickly than she would have expected. Trying to knit made her feel as if she were all thumbs, but she enjoyed spending time with Jenny and Lizzie. It made her all the more aware of how caught up in work she had been in her own time, both with her teaching and with trying to get gigs. Working evenings and weekends had left her little time for a social life, and her friendships had suffered.

"We don't always go to the dance," Jenny said, "but sometimes Eli allows it. He finds it rather frivolous, but it's one of the better ways for Lizzie and the boys to meet other young people. And he knows I still sometimes miss Kentucky. I had friends there and there were more places to socialize."

Tori thought Eli sounded like a regular tyrant, and had to remind herself that roles were very different for women in this time. "Surely there's nothing wrong with a little entertainment."

"I don't think so, but Eli takes a more serious view of life."

"Well, I am looking forward to going," Tori said, realizing somewhat to her surprise that this was true.

Jenny smiled. "I've noticed how you brighten up every time it's mentioned. I suspect it has something to do with the young man who is taking you."

"Sebastien? No, I barely know him." Tori could feel the heat stealing up her cheeks.

"But he's handsome?"

"Very." Tori considered his deep-set blue eyes, compact well-muscled body, and steely jaw. She did not doubt that all the other women at the dance would envy her.

Jenny leaned close and whispered so her daughter couldn't hear. "I think Lizzie has her eye on our neighbors' son. It would be a good match."

Tori dropped a stitch and bit off an unladylike response. Lizzie seemed far too young to marry. She set aside her knitting in disgust.

"Don't fret." Jenny reached for Tori's needles and deftly fixed her mistake. "It takes a while to learn."

Tori glanced over at Lizzie and wondered how old she was. Girls married much earlier in this time. She supposed she herself could be considered an old maid, still unwed at the ripe old age of twenty-three.

"Why don't you go upstairs and rest until it's time to get ready. You, too, Lizzie."

Lizzie quickly set aside the hat she was knitting before her mother could change her mind. "Come on," she said to Tori and led the way up the ladder.

Tori removed her hideous gray dress and curled up under the blankets. She would rest a few minutes, then change into something more festive for the dance.

* * *

"Time to get ready." Someone shook her shoulder.

Tori opened her eyes to the gloom of candlelight and Lizzie standing over her. She must have fallen asleep. Lizzie returned to her side of the attic, and Tori dressed in the same outfit she'd worn for her violin performance the night she'd been thrown back in time. She thought it the most attractive of her limited options. She could hear Lizzie and her oldest brother, Seth, changing as well. Tori brushed her hair and wound it up in a knot on the back of her head. She recalled how Anne had helped her with her hair that fateful night. Her friend would be surprised by how easily she accomplished the style now. She grabbed her coat and climbed down the ladder.

Jenny, dressed in a printed cotton gown with lace at the neck and sleeves, outshone both her guest and her daughter. "Eli is going to stay home with Mark. He's a bit young to come."

A knock on the door announced the arrival of Sebastien and Roger. Both men had exchanged their leather pants and jackets for breeches and boots, topped with evening coats. Tori's eyes widened as she realized that Sebastien had even shaved his beard, highlighting the strength of his jawline and sharp cheekbones.

Sebastien offered her his arm, while Roger took Mrs. Sellers'. Seth was left to escort his sister, which he did after making a face.

"Don't be out too late," Eli said, frowning at the sight of his wife's hand on the middle-aged keelboater's arm. In her other hand, she carried an apple pie to contribute to the spread. Tori kept her face expressionless, but inwardly she smiled at Eil's disgruntled face. If he had realized how well the boatmen cleaned up, he might not have given his wife permission to go to the dance.

They walked briskly to the barn where the dance was held. The weather was mild for December, but still cold, especially to Tori who missed central heating. She held back as they reached the building and allowed the others to go inside.

"What's wrong?" Sebastien asked.

Tori chewed on her lip. She had wanted to see him all day and get his advice about how to prepare for the earthquake, but now that he was here, she didn't know how to approach him either. "I think something bad is going to happen. Tonight. I want to warn people, but I don't know how."

He frowned. "Why would you think this?"

"I had a strange dream last night. I think it was a premonition." She expected Sebastien to laugh at her, but he seemed to take her words seriously.

"What did you dream?"

"The ground was shaking and the walls of the house were collapsing around us."

"You have been through a lot in the past week. I think such a dream is perfectly normal, and might mean nothing."

At least he considered her theory. "I've felt uneasy for several days."

"I don't think you need to worry. Come, let's dance."

Tori allowed him to lead her inside the building. She didn't know what else to do. "Are you staying on the *Fury*?"

"Of course."

Many lives had been lost on the river. "I think you should take a room for the night."

Now he laughed. "And have the walls fall down about my ears?"

"Better that than drowning!"

The humor fled from his face. "You really believe something will happen. Have you warned the Sellerses?"

"No. I was afraid they would think me crazy."

"Jenny might listen to you, but it would be best if you said nothing to Eli."

Tori agreed. "I suppose we might as well dance. We can't change the future." At least she didn't think they could. Or should. She'd seen enough time travel movies to know that if she messed something up in this time line, it might threaten her existence. She gazed around the room and tried to relax.

Sebastien took her coat and placed it on a table with the others. It stood out, sitting upon a pile of furs and woolen jackets, but so far the Sellerses had not commented on it. The sounds of conversation and laughter filled the air along with that of the musicians warming up. She noted the fiddler, an older gentleman with a bit of a belly, but a light touch on his instrument. There was also a piano player and a few instruments she couldn't identify.

> 101

In another corner of the room a makeshift bar served drinks. Sebastien led her to it, and got them each a glass of amber liquid.

"What is it?" Tori asked as she took a sniff. Her eyes watered.

"Good Kentucky whiskey," Sebastien said, amusement lighting his eyes at her reaction. He swallowed a healthy portion. "Try it."

"I usually don't drink strong alcohol. Your men drink it all the time, but I just don't see the attraction."

"It helps keep the cold at bay."

Well, that makes it more tempting. Tori sampled a mouthful. As she had guessed from the smell, it was strong, burning its way down to her stomach. But it was pleasant for all that, especially the tendrils of warmth it sent throughout her body.

Another table groaned under the weight of food set up on it. Tori saw pies, both sweet and savory, platters of bread, cheese and cold meat and a few dishes she didn't recognize. The people gathered around the table were dressed in a rainbow of colors, a vivid contrast from the grim bunch she had gone to church with that morning. The colors weren't as bright as she was used to in her own time, since they were probably dyed from natural ingredients, but they still appeared festive.

Most of the people spoke French, so Tori couldn't understand them, but she was glad to see that many of the crew members were present, both the men she knew from the *Fury* and those she knew only by sight, from the *Revenge*.

As the music began, people took the floor. The boatmen snatched up the pretty girls, leaving many of the local men without partners. They stood on the sidelines, brooding, glasses of whiskey in their hands. Seth was without a partner, but he seemed to take it in stride, carrying a heaping plate of food over to one of the chairs and digging in.

"Shall we?" Sebastien asked.

Tori gulped the rest of her drink as she gazed out at the dancers. They weren't just gyrating to the music any old way they wanted.

They moved together, in specified motions, in a way that reminded Tori of a square dance. "I'm afraid I don't know how to dance."

Sebastien raised a brow. "I might expect that from an ignorant country girl, but not from an Easterner."

"I am usually playing the fiddle, not dancing, so I never learned."

"I will have to teach you. There are too few girls here to allow one to sit on the sideline."

The alcohol swirling in her blood gave her courage, but she still found the idea terrifying. "I couldn't," she said stepping away from him.

Sebastien took the empty glass from her nerveless fingers. "Of course you can. We won't join a set until you are ready, but I will show you the steps. None of them are hard."

Might as well. What did it matter, if they were all to be killed by an earthquake tonight? Tori's hand trembled in Sebastien's grip. She reminded herself that there had been few, if any, fatalities in New Madrid from the first quake. Records of the time period were far from perfect, but Anne had explained to her that most of those killed had died on the river. Many of those deaths had gone undocumented, as had the deaths of Native Americans and others who lived in isolated areas.

When she thought of the devastation to come, the possibility of making a fool of herself on the dance floor seemed trivial. So she did her best to follow Sebastien's guidance. It was not as hard as she would have thought. She found it difficult to remember all the steps and the order they went in, but the movements themselves followed the rhythm of the music and once she got the hang of a series of steps, she glided through them effortlessly.

"You are doing very well. Are you sure you've never danced before?"

"I didn't say I had never danced, just that I didn't know how to do *these* dances."

"With all the travelers passing through, New Madrid prides itself on keeping up to date on Eastern customs. If you know new dances, teach them to me."

Tori laughed. She knew new dances all right, but didn't think she should show Sebastien how to do the Macarena. "No, that's not what I meant. I was talking about dancing around the room, just for fun."

Sebastien gave her a strange look. "You dance around the room by yourself? Without music?"

Well, no I usually play something from my iPod. "Why not?"

"No reason. Do you feel up to joining a set?"

"Why not?" she repeated. "But can I have another drink first?"

"You'll be tipsy."

"All the better."

Sebastien bought her another drink. After a few fortifying sips, Tori felt ready to take on the challenge. They joined a set and she did her best to follow Sebastien's whispered instructions. She faltered when they changed partners, but her new partner, one of Sebastien's crew, didn't seem to mind when she went in the wrong direction or even when she stepped on his feet. Since she wore the slippers she had found in Ste. Genevieve, her false moves did him no damage; however, when his booted foot stepped on her toes, the stabbing pain forced her off the dance floor.

"I'm sorry, Miss Victoria," her partner said, shamefaced.

"It's fine. I stepped on your foot first."

"You're not a big brute and you're not wearing boots."

Tori winced and rubbed at her throbbing toes. "I'll be all right. But could you bring me my drink? It's over there." She pointed to where she had left her whiskey. He fetched it for her and she sipped at it, watching the dancers continue on without them. "You don't have to stay with me."

"Might as well. No one left to dance with."

"True enough." She kept her eye on Sebastien and his partner. Neither were the best dancers in the room, although they knew the steps better than Tori, but Sebastien smiled as he spun her around and she beamed as if she had won the lottery. The girl's excitement resonated with Tori. Sebastien was the most handsome man in the room. And despite having been born in the eighteenth century, he never dismissed her out of hand. While he didn't believe in her "prophetic" dream, he also didn't discount it.

Her toe-smashing partner wandered off to the bar and Bob Rivers, "the Rattler," took his place. "Have your feet recovered enough from the abuse of your previous partners to manage the next set?"

Her toes still hurt, but the fierce pain had subsided. With the lack of female partners, she felt churlish sitting out. "I'm game, but I warn you that I'm not a good dancer."

"Excellent." He stepped closer, like a dog guarding a bone.

Tori stifled a flicker of uneasiness. She knew Sebastien didn't fully trust the man and her own instincts made her wary as well, but what harm could he do her in a room full of people? She wouldn't go outside with him. Allowing Mr. Henderson to catch her alone had been her undoing. "What drew you to the river trade. Were you a trapper like Sebastien?"

An expression she couldn't interpret darted across his face. "Heavens, no. My father is in trade back East and I'm following in his footsteps. I don't plan to captain a keelboat all my life. Once I've saved up enough money to buy some property, I'll settle here, unless I go back East."

He might be stuck on the river for longer than he intended, Tori thought, knowing something of the chaos to come. If he lost his boat in the quakes, he could end up bankrupt. "With a name like 'the Rattler,' I would think you'd be fond of adventure. It's hard to picture you as a farmer."

"Looks can be deceiving, and I've had enough adventure to last me a lifetime."

Tori got the impression he had flipped the conversation over to her. None of the people she'd met in either Ste. Genevieve or New

Madrid had questioned her story, but these river men sure were suspicious. Sebastien as well, though he kept his doubts to himself. "A new set is forming. Shall we join in?"

Rat took her hand. He moved with authority, nearly dragging her through the parts where she hesitated. Tori appreciated the help even as she resented his bossiness.

"Why don't you know how to dance? Family too religious?"

"No, I just usually provide the music."

Rat barked a laugh. "Thought that couldn't be Dalton playing the other night. That was you?"

Tori nodded.

Rat chuckled. "Bet Sebastien loved that. You should have let me take you on board. I appreciate a well-played melody."

"Why doesn't Sebastien like music?"

He shrugged. "He's a trapper. His father was a trapper. You can't expect culture from men like that."

Tori frowned. Sebastien might not have a love of art or music, but he had treated her well. "He has behaved like a perfect gentleman, even though I more or less forced him into taking me on as a passenger."

"I find that fascinating," Rat said, his eyes narrowed on his fellow keelboat operator. "It's out of character for men who live rough on the river to deny their instincts. Trust me, he will expect to be compensated for his effort."

That twinge of guilt reared its ugly head again, but she sensed an animosity between the two men and didn't think their opinions of one another were credible. She tried to think of something else to discuss that was less controversial, but Rat beat her.

"What are your thoughts on the comet? Do you think it a bad omen like most of the superstitious fools around here?"

"Actually, I do, and I don't consider myself a fool. You would do well to heed its warning."

"Might signal a major Indian uprising," he allowed, "but only because they, too, think it's some sort of sign."

By the time the dance ended, Tori's annoyance had grown. Although he danced well and didn't spit or swear like the hired men, his arrogance surpassed even Mr. Henderson's.

Sebastien claimed her for the next set. "Would you like to sit this one out and get something to eat?"

"That sounds great."

They walked over to the food tables and began filling their plates. Sebastien also refilled their drinks. "Are you enjoying yourself?"

She took a swallow of whiskey. "Yes, even though my feet have been stepped on and my ideas insulted."

"Rivers?"

"Who else? He thinks everyone who believes the comet is a bad omen is a superstitious fool."

"Did you tell him about your dream?"

"Of course not." She almost felt he deserved to be swallowed by the river.

When they finished eating, Sebastien fetched her coat and took her outside. The comet blazed across the sky, its forked tail vaguely ominous. Tori shivered. Knowing what she did, it was hard to believe it wasn't a bad omen.

"Are you cold?"

"I'm fine." She sat next to him on a bench and allowed him to put his arm around her. "Have you been to many of these dances?"

"A few. The men like to blow off steam, but they only have them on Sundays."

She was glad that she had come, that he had brought her. In her own time it seemed like women had to beg men to get them to dance, so she had found it refreshing to be in demand. But dancing with Sebastien had been special, and not only because he'd demonstrated the steps. Her attraction to him went beyond the physical. Maybe Rat was right, and Sebastien was helping her only to get his hands on her necklace, but Tori could not believe that. If she had met him in her own time, she would have wanted to date him. He was so different from worms like Ned, and jerks like her boss at the studio and Mr. Henderson.

She closed her eyes when Sebastien moved in for a kiss. His lips were warm against hers and tasted of whiskey. He drew her in close and she wished she could rid herself of the bulk of her coat. She longed to be held against his powerful chest, to feel his heart beating. It was too cold to remove the coat entirely, but she hadn't zipped it up, so the front fell open as she snuggled closer. If only she could stay here and not worry about returning to her own time or being swallowed up by an earthquake.

Sebastien nuzzled at her ear and a sensual shiver slid down her spine. "I told myself I wouldn't do this, but you're too tempting."

Tori mumbled in reply. He smelled of the river, cold and dark, and the musky scent of male. She squashed a hint of misgiving. Sebastien was not Ned. He wasn't collecting payment. This was mutual, something they both desired.

"Seeing you aboard the *Fury* every day… well, that's another reason why I don't take on passengers."

"I've done my best to not cause trouble," she said, but she knew what he meant. Seeing Sebastien every day, his confident stride and assertive command, had made her hungry for this moment.

He drew back far enough to look her in the eyes. His were serious and dark with desire. "I'm a river man."

"I know that," she replied, although she had the feeling she had missed something.

"Well, then…" He brushed a tendril of hair from her face that had escaped from her chignon. He kissed her again—hard, the built-up passion between them igniting as he slipped his hands inside her coat and ran them up the back of her dress. She did the same, slipping her hands under his dress coat and along his shirt. Too many layers.

They necked like teenagers on that cold hard bench for what seemed like hours, but couldn't have been more than a few minutes. Sebastien ended it, pulling away when her fingers brushed along the ridge standing out from his breeches.

"Forgive me. I got carried away."

"Me, too." Tori blushed as she realized that anyone could have come out from the party at any time and seen their passionate embrace.

"I should take you home. Mrs. Sellers and her children left a few hours ago."

Tori agreed, for she had no desire to return to the dance and stumble through another set. She zipped up her coat as Sebastien ducked inside for a torch to light their way. When he returned with the burning brand, she offered him a smile.

"We won't leave until later in the morning. The men will be worthless at sunrise. I'll send Roger to get you."

You probably won't leave at all. She made a sound of assent, but while she'd put aside her worries during the dance, now they were back full force. The stars shone brightly overhead, and the torch threw menacing shadows in their path. They might not have needed it at all, but there was no moon. The light of the torch and the stars were all that lit the way, although Tori had not yet become accustomed to how bright the night sky appeared in this century. Once she glimpsed the Sellerses' house at a distance, she knew her time with Sebastien was nearly over. She savored the feel of his hand in hers even though they had both donned their gloves for the walk. "Be careful," she said as they stood on the porch. The house was mostly dark, but a single candle burned in the kitchen, left, she was sure, for her convenience.

"Always." He brushed his lips against hers. "I will see you tomorrow."

He waited while she slipped inside and grabbed the candle. She carefully made her way up to the loft, one hand on the ladder rungs

> 109

and the other gripping her light source. She removed her clothes, slipped into bed and blew out the candle. She knew she wouldn't sleep a wink.

Chapter 13

A roaring sound like a train tore through the house and shook it on its foundation. Tori gasped and clung to the bed frame as it bucked like a bronco, trying to throw her out. Behind the partition, the children screamed and she heard Eli and Jenny crying out downstairs.

Dishes shattered and objects fell to the floor. The floor tilted and Tori's bed slid sideways, tearing through the quilt and crashing into the other beds. It was very dark, but she heard one of the children fall out of bed and land on the floor. She reached for her necklace, pulling it free of her nightdress. She couldn't see anything in the pitch blackness, but it did not warm to her touch, nor did it glow.

"What's going on?" Lizzie asked.

"It's an earthquake," Tori said. "Grab something warm. We need to get out of the house." She slipped out of bed, only partly by her own volition. She tried to walk back to her side of the attic for her boots and coat, but the floor rolled beneath her feet. Falling, she proceeded on hands and knees, searching all the while for her boots. She had left them right by the bed in preparation for a hasty exit, but had underestimated the force of the quake. They could have gone anywhere.

"It's dark, I can't see," moaned Mark, the youngest.

"'Course you can't see, it's nighttime," his brother shot back.

"Seth, Lizzie, Mark—are you all right?" Jenny shouted up at the attic.

"Help, Ma! I fell out of bed and can't see nothing."

"Stay put. Don't try to come down the ladder," Eli's voice cut through his son's whining. "This should be over in a minute."

In the darkness, Tori's hand touched a boot and she grabbed on to it like a lifeline, shoving her foot inside. She spread her arms wide, hoping the other boot would be nearby. Just as her fingers encountered the familiar fluffy warmth, the floor ceased buckling beneath her and the house seemed to lurch back into position. She took a deep breath as relief washed over her. They were done. For now.

Eli had managed to light a lantern and he came up to the top of the ladder. The light provided a comforting glow. "Anyone hurt?"

"I banged my elbow, Pa, and Seth stepped on me."

"I didn't mean to. I couldn't see you."

"Stop your fussing. Miss Foster, you doing all right?"

"Yes, but we should bundle up and head outside."

"The house survived. All the walls are still standing. It's mighty cold outside. We'll stay here until morning and then check for damage."

"I don't think it's safe to stay in the house, Mr. Sellers. There might be aftershocks."

Eli gave her an angry look. "What's an aftershock?"

Guess the word's not yet in use. "Additional, smaller earthquakes."

"If you're worried about so-called 'aftershocks,' you're free to leave at any time, but I decide what is best for my family."

Tori clenched her hands to keep from slapping him. Instead, she took advantage of the light to find her coat and pull it over her flannel nightdress.

"Go back to bed. You have school tomorrow," Eli said.

Tori rolled her eyes. School was probably over for the rest of the year. She climbed down the ladder in Eli's wake. Jenny stood in the ruins of her kitchen, dish fragments all around, a robe thrown over her night clothes. "Are you sure you want to go outside?" she asked. "It's very cold."

"I think it best." As if to accent her words, a tremor shook the house and Jenny stifled a scream.

She looked over at her husband. "Eli?"

"That wasn't so bad. We stay."

"At least let the children come down. What if the roof caves in?"

Eli grunted, which Jenny must have taken as assent, for she called out for the children to come downstairs. "Bring your blankets and curl up on the floor."

Tori slipped outside as Mark scrambled down the ladder and launched himself into his mother's arms. It was very dark outside and cold, as the Sellerses had warned her. Only a faint outline of the comet lingered in the sky, and even the stars appeared muted. She wasn't the only one to seek sanctuary in the open. Several other families had left their houses and stood in disarray in the street. She could just make out their shapes in the dark. No one appeared seriously hurt.

She caught snatches of conversations and heard the word "earthquake" bandied around. A few seemed to think the quake was the disaster the comet had foretold, while others said it was the wrath of God for sinful activities—like drinking and dancing on a Sunday.

Someone dragged some wood into a pile and started a fire. People gathered around its warmth, including Tori, though she kept to the edge, not wanting to intrude where she might not be wanted. Someone, who knew where she was lodging, asked about the Sellerses.

"They're fine. They decided to stay in their house for the night."

"I told you we should stay," the wife told her husband. "We'll catch our death out here."

"Stay by the fire. Until we get a good look at the house, we don't know whether it's safe to go back."

Grumbling, the woman obeyed, moving closer to the flames. She fell silent as another tremor caused the earth to shift beneath their feet.

Tori wondered what was happening at the river, but was afraid to trek down there in the unnatural gloom. A foul odor seeped into the air, giving weight to the arguments that the earthquake was a punishment from God.

"Smells like hellfire, don't it?" said one of the doom-and-gloomers. "Told you this was the devil's work."

She scooted away from the hellfire dude and asked another group of survivors if they had seen any of the boatman or knew anything about conditions on the river, but no one had ventured that far.

"Thought I heard the bank cave in," one person said. "We lose part of the town every year. Used to be a fort here when this was Spanish land, but it's long gone."

Tori's breath caught in her throat. She hoped Sebastien and his crew were all right. She even hoped that no harm had come to Rat and his gang.

She was tired, having only slept two hours or so before the quake struck—although she hadn't expected to sleep at all. She curled up against a log and felt for the necklace under her clothes. *Still there and still nothing more than a lifeless stone.* She lay her head in her arms and nodded off after a while. She heard people come and go, their conversations washing over her head. She was cold and uncomfortable, but no one tried to chase her away from the fire. It was still dark when the second major quake struck.

Chapter 14

Sebastien awoke in the middle of the night when a massive wave lifted and dropped the *Fury* like a child with a paper boat, and tossed him out of bed. Used to responding quickly, he was awake before he hit the floor with a painful thud. He ran out of the cabin to find it dark as pitch on deck. Roger and his men soon joined him.

"What the hell is going on?" one of the men asked.

The *Fury* bobbed in the river, which frothed and churned like the ocean. The earth roared and spat. A blast of steam burst from the riverbed not three feet from where they were moored, shooting water up in the air like a geyser. A few of the men screamed and even in the dark, Sebastien saw Roger hastily cross himself.

"Earthquake," he said. *How did she know?* Had she really had a prophetic dream? His mother had believed in such things—in shamans and soothsayers. As he grew older, he'd dismissed his mother's tales, and although he'd listened to Victoria, he did not believe people were capable of seeing into the future.

"Earthquake? Then why is the river moving?"

"There is land beneath the water," Sebastien said. The river surged again, carrying the boat with it and then dropping it once more. The rope that held them to the shore strained, but held. "Cut us loose."

"Patron? Are you certain?"

Roger drew close. "I don't think we can navigate these waters, Sebastien," he said in a low voice.

"We can't, but we're too vulnerable tethered to the ground. I'd rather take our chances on the water."

The men stood by nervously, not leaping to obey their orders as they normally did.

"You heard the man," Roger yelled. "Cut the damn rope!"

This time they moved, sawing through the hemp as the boat bucked and kicked in protest. At last they were free and drifting out into the river. "Try to keep her steady, men," Sebastien called and they grabbed their poles, trying to keep to the center of the river and away from the banks. A nauseous stink filled the air, worse than that of the decaying vegetation they were accustomed to, and made it difficult to breathe. The lack of a moon made it difficult to see anything, particularly obstacles in the water. They drifted downstream trying only to stay afloat.

Rivers cut loose moments after they did, but Sebastien soon lost sight of the other boat in the ominous darkness. A crashing sound signaled the collapse of a bank and water surged over the bow as tons of earth, trees and all, tumbled into the river. "Hold up!" he yelled and the men dug their poles into the river bottom, keeping the boat from running in to the debris that blocked their path.

The dull rumbling which had served as the backdrop to the river shenanigans, died off. Roger made his way to Sebastien. "Is it over?"

"Sounds like. Not sure if we're out of danger, though."

"Should we head back to shore? Half the men are still in New Madrid, as well as our lovely passenger."

Sebastien scowled. He really needed to talk to Victoria. Then, to his annoyance, he found himself worrying about how bad the situation was on land. What if the Sellerses' house had fallen down? He might never get the chance to ask how she had known about the earthquakes. "We'll tie up for the rest of the night, avoiding high ground. There could be aftershocks and more banks could go."

Roger relayed his instructions to the men and they poled their way back to shore. It took a few tries before they found a spot that suited Sebastien. The river still churned and the stink had worsened.

"Men, I need a few of you to stay on board, but the rest of you can take your bedrolls over to shore if you feel more secure there." Most of the crew chose to remain on board, but a few camped out on the shore. A tremor hit as they made their way over and one changed his mind, deciding to stick with the river.

"Ground shook like a jelly," he said when he climbed back on the boat. "I want no part of that."

"Get what rest you can," Sebastien advised. "We don't know what tomorrow will bring."

* * *

Sebastien spent the night on deck. He dozed fitfully, but never fully slept. He guessed from the motion of the river that additional tremors struck, but nothing compelled him to leave shore again. Dawn was just beginning to peek over the horizon when a second quake hit.

The earth roared like a bear and the faint glow of the sun captured the sight of trees swaying as if in a stiff breeze. The men who had stayed on board came running and Sebastien could hear those who had gone ashore screaming in terror.

Roger, white-faced, appeared at his side. "Cut free?"

"Do it."

The hands rushed to free the boat and pole toward the center of the river. The earth heaved and the river shook in response, rising and falling and at times appearing to rush backward. A tree, buried deep beneath the water, tore loose and shot into the air, landing on the eastern bank. The men fought to keep the boat afloat as waves tried to swamp it. At last the noise receded, the trees stood still, and the river regained some of its calm.

"Damage report?" Sebastien called out.

Men scurried around the boat checking seams and masts. Nothing seemed to be damaged. "We need to pick up the men on shore and then head back to New Madrid," Sebastien told his crew. He wasn't sure how far they had drifted during the first quake, but the second quake had carried them several hundred feet.

The men set to work poling back to their landing place. Poling against the current was brutally hard work at any time. Dealing with strange ebbs and the volume of new trees choking the river made the task even more difficult.

When they arrived at their camping spot, the men were waiting for them. "A crack opened in the earth not far from where we were sleeping," one of the men said. "Had it been a few feet over, we'd have been goners for sure."

"How deep was it?"

"You think I checked? Smelled like hell itself. Something black came out of it. I got as far away as I could."

Sebastien frowned. "Listen up. We're short-handed, but we need to get back to New Madrid as soon as possible. We need to pick up the rest of the crew and Miss Foster. We lost contact with the *Revenge*, but hopefully we'll meet back up. Seems like our trip to New Orleans is not going to be the smooth sailing we're used to." He told Roger to take the roof and joined his men, putting shoulder to the poles and forcing the boat upstream. In places where the water was too deep for poling, they used the cordelle, a towline several hundred feet long which the men would take ashore and tromp through the brush, pulling the boat behind them. They passed a few wrecks, some seemingly undamaged but drifting empty of crew. Others were little more than splintered husks, jagged ribs sticking out of the water as they floated by.

Progress was slow, but they didn't have far to go and it was still morning when they returned to their mooring space. The first sight of the town, although sobering, eased Sebastien's fears. He noted that most of the houses had lost their chimneys, but none had collapsed. His fellow boatmen, who had not cut loose, had fared worse. At least one had been crushed by a falling bank and several others were stranded in the bayou. The rapid rise of water had carried them up the smaller stream, trapping them when the water receded.

Roger whistled at the sight. "Good thing we got out fast."

"Doubt even horses could pull them free."

"You'd best go see if she's all right."

"Miss Foster is hellbent on making it to New Orleans. I guess I should put her mind at rest." Sebastien gave orders to his crew, telling some to stay and watch the boat and others to go in search of their comrades. He headed toward the Sellerses' house, but before he could reach it, he found the bulk of the townspeople gathered outside by a roaring bonfire. He began searching for Victoria.

She spotted him first. "Sebastien," she cried out and dashed across the street. "I've been so worried. No one had news of either the *Fury* or the *Revenge*."

"We cut loose when the quake struck and took our chances with the river. The *Revenge* did as well, but we haven't seen them yet today." He decided not to tell her about the empty and ruined boats they had seen. She would find out for herself soon enough.

"I came out here after the first quake. The Sellerses stayed behind, but abandoned the house after the second large one."

"Any casualties?"

"One woman is said to have died of fright. She had no obvious injuries. The rest are mostly cuts and bruises."

"I'm gathering up my crew and we'll depart as soon as possible. Is it safe for you to go back into the Sellerses' house and get your things?"

"I think so, but... you're continuing down the river? Do you have any idea how dangerous that is?"

"I had a taste last night." He glared at her, his temper not improved from his sleepless night. "We need to talk. Let's go to the Sellerses' place." He strode away without looking back. After a few minutes, he could hear the soft scuffle of her boots as she followed.

The door hung at an angle from its frame, but a glance around the inside showed no immediate danger. "Come in. I don't want to be overheard."

Tori stepped tentatively across the threshold. "My things are upstairs."

"They can wait." He drew her over to the parlor. A layer of dust had fallen from the ceiling and covered the sofa. They brushed it off before sitting. "I want to know how you knew about the earthquake."

"I told you. I had a dream." Her clear blue eyes met his straight on.

Could she be telling the truth? "Does everything you dream about come true?"

"Of course not. But there were other signs, like the comet."

"The comet has been around for months."

"I only had the dream a couple days ago. And then there were the animals."

Sebastien frowned.

"The Sellers boys were talking about how strange the animals were behaving when they went out hunting. Only then did I put everything together."

Sebastien's mother had looked to animals for information about the future. When the pelts of the creatures they trapped were especially thick, she prepared for a long, hard winter. Most of the time, her preparation paid off. She always claimed that animals had ways of knowing things that humans did not. He still felt that Victoria was hiding something, but what had he expected her to say? Did he suspect her of dabbling in magic? Did he think her somehow responsible for the earthquake? He had to admit that her story was far more logical than his crazy suspicions. "Have you ever had a dream that came true before this?"

Victoria shook her head. "Never. I don't have the Sight, but maybe, like the animals, I sensed something most people did not."

She spoke easily about the Sight without crossing herself, as many people Sebastien knew would have done. "Do you believe in the Sight?"

"A week ago, I would have said 'no,' but now I think anything is possible."

"Since you fell into the river?"

"I should be dead, but you saved me."

The light shining in her eyes made him uncomfortable. "I got lucky."

"No," she said softly. "I was the lucky one."

Chapter 15

Tori searched for the Sellerses to say her farewells and wish them good luck. The ground continued to shake periodically, and a few houses had sustained greater damage than just their chimneys falling down. Deciding it was unsafe to return to the mostly wooden structures, the townspeople had set about building a bunch of tents at the edge of the settlement to house the residents until the tremors ceased.

"Jenny, I'm getting ready to leave, but wanted to thank you for your hospitality."

Jenny stared at her, her face pale. "We're going to be moving into a temporary structure. In winter!"

Tori scuffed at the dirt with her foot. "I heard." She felt bad for the townspeople, especially since she knew they would never move back into their rustic, but cozy, cabins.

"I can't do it, Victoria. This is the last straw for me. I've tried my best to be a good wife, but I can't stand it any more. I'm going to ask Sebastien to take me and Lizzie with him when he goes. The boys can stay with their father."

"Sebastien doesn't usually take on passengers. He made an exception for me." *Reluctantly.*

"I still have some of my dowry money and family in Virginia willing to take us in. The earthquake may have forced my hand, but this will work out better for you as well. You shouldn't be traveling alone with all those men. Your reputation will be in shreds by the time you reach New Orleans."

Tori had grown comfortable with most of the rough-hewn men, though there were still a few she gave a wide berth to. She realized her unchaperoned state was scandalous for the time, but couldn't bring herself to worry about it when larger issues were at stake—like survival and finding a way home. "I really applied a lot of pressure to get Sebastien to take me. I don't think he'll agree to take on any more passengers."

"You leave that to me."

Tori climbed aboard the *Fury* with some trepidation, but what else was she to do? Stay in the tent city in New Madrid? She had hoped the earthquake might trigger the necklace, but since it hadn't, she would continue with her plan. She only hoped the *Fury* could make the hazardous journey safely.

She had barely stored her meager possessions in Sebastien's cabin when, to her surprise, Jenny entered, a trunk in each hand.

"Sebastien agreed to take you on?"

"I offered him a tempting sum and appealed to his compassion and sense of propriety.

Sebastien had a sense of propriety? Tori suppressed a giggle. "I thought he would refuse."

Jenny smiled. "I enlisted Roger's help. Sebastien usually stays on board the *Fury*, but Roger has stayed with me in the past and didn't want to leave me here under these conditions."

"What about Lizzie?" Tori eyed the small space and single bunk.

Jenny's face hardened. "Eli would have let me take her, but she wants to stay here because of that stupid boy. I almost brought Mark, but at the last minute Eli decided he couldn't spare him." Her lips compressed together and her warm brown eyes held a sheen of moisture.

Tori swallowed. She guessed that men held all the power in custody disputes in the nineteenth century. She was surprised that Jenny, who appeared to be a loving mother, would leave her children, but her only other choice was to stay here in New Madrid, braving the winter in a tent. "I'm sorry you have to leave your children behind."

"I might be able to send for them later. At least for a visit..." Her voice trailed off and her shoulders slumped. Then she straightened. "Or perhaps I will come back in the spring, after they have time to rebuild. In the meantime, I'm looking forward to taking you under my wing. Despite being raised in the East, you don't seem to have learned all you should know about being a lady."

"It might be best to stick to knitting."

"There will be time for that as well," Jenny promised. The two women left the cabin and returned to the deck, where the crew prepared to set off.

A couple of the men had fled during the night, but most returned to the boat. The women listened to the men who had been on land swapping stories with those who had been on the river. Sebastien met with the captains of the stranded boats and agreed to buy some of their more valuable cargo. It worked out favorably for each party. Sebastien got a deal on the goods, and the other captains recouped some of their investment.

Once the new cargo was loaded, they set off. Tori and Jenny sat with Sebastien up on the roof of the cabin. A group of townspeople, including Jenny's children, waved them off. There was no sign of Eli.

They didn't travel far before the devastation caused by the earthquakes became apparent. Remnants of swamped boats drifted aimlessly, along with their ruined cargo. Trees clogged the waterway, making it more difficult than ever to navigate.

"The river has changed course here," Sebastien said, pointing to where it used to flow. His eagle eyes came in handy, but his memory of the river and his guidebook were less useful, as they continued to encounter change.

Tori, who had been afraid to get back on the boat because she recalled Anne telling her that there had been more deaths on the river than on land, began to see the evidence of this. "The quakes were terrifying on land, but what happened on the river to cause so many boats to sink?"

"There were waves higher than those on the ocean. Or, at least I assume they were. I've never sailed on the ocean, though I've a mind to someday."

Tori's mother had taken her on a cruise as a high school graduation gift. Sunning herself by the pool, eating delicious meals and listening to music or going to shows at night had been the perfect relaxation after the whirlwind of activity of her senior year. "I have."

"Did your theatrical group tour Europe?" Sebastien asked.

"No, my mother took me on a trip to the West Indies before I started performing."

"I plan to catch a ship to the East Coast once we reach New Orleans," Jenny said.

"I've met men who take ships from New Orleans to the islands and then up the East Coast. They say the West Indies are very beautiful." Sebastien sounded wistful.

"But you've never gone yourself?"

"No, I'd need an ocean-going vessel. One of these days I'll take the *Fury* up the Ohio, maybe go as far as Pittsburgh, but so far I've stuck with what I know."

"The islands are lovely, but there is a lot of poverty there."

"As well as great wealth," Sebastien added.

Tori made a noncommittal noise. She supposed in this time, there were a number of wealthy plantation owners living in Bahamas.

"Don't forget the constant threat of slave uprisings," Jenny said.

Tori sat up straighter. She hadn't thought about the fact that she was now living in pre-Civil War times. Everything seemed so strange to her that she hadn't really noticed that she had seen very few African-American people. There had been the doctor's servant girl, whom May had sent to the riverfront with Tori's message for Sebastien, in Ste. Genevieve and a few black people gathered around the fire in New Madrid, but it had never occurred to her that they might be slaves. There was a lot of racial tension in her time, but here, with slavery and the possibility of Indian attacks, things were much worse.

Sebastien kept a careful eye on the river, mainly to avoid collisions, but he also took the time to investigate promising cargo. Most was waterlogged and unusable, but on occasion he fished something out that he thought he could dry off and sell in New Orleans. Steering toward one such possibility, they discovered a man clinging to the box. They hauled him on board, reminding Tori of her own rescue.

"Are you all right, mister?"

"Boat sank," the man muttered. "Trees fell, we tipped over. Water everywhere."

"Are there any other survivors?"

"Don't know. Thought I was dead, but the Mississippi spit me out. I found this box and held on."

"Roger, take him to our cabin and see if you can find him some dry clothes. Jenny, do you think you could make us all some hot coffee?"

Jenny nodded. "Give me a hand," she said to Tori, and Tori realized she would no longer be allowed to spend time alone with Sebastien.

A handful of braziers burned on deck. They provided warmth and were used by the men to heat the occasional snack, but the majority of the cooking was done on a rudimentary wood stove at the end of the cabin section. Tori had not yet tried to use it, but surely she could boil some water, grind some coffee beans, and mix the two together. She and Jenny slid off the roof and entered the cabin area from the rear. A kettle of water was always kept going on the stove, but Jenny opened the door at the front of the stove and used a poker to stir up the wood. A black box with a handle stood nearby, and Tori tossed a couple handfuls of beans into it from a large bag resting on the floor.

She'd watched Roger make coffee in the mornings, so she turned the handle until she had a fine powder.

When Jenny brought the water over, it seemed hot enough, but it wasn't boiling. Tori would have preferred boiling, for safety reasons, but hoped the strong coffee would kill any bacteria in the water. She filled the coffee pot and they took it out on deck.

The rescued man had been given dry clothes and a warm blanket, just as she had been. As he warmed up, he grew more coherent and they learned he had been part of a flatboat crew hauling a load of salt pork to New Orleans.

"Thanks for saving me. I tried to kick to shore, but the current was too strong." He took another sip of coffee. "Did you feel those waves? At first, with all the noise, we thought it was Indians. We all grabbed our guns and prepared to fight, but there was nothing to shoot at. We were tied up on the bank, but there was a landslide and a bunch of trees came tumbling into the river, knocking us over. I've seen landslides before, but nothing like this. It all happened so sudden-like and there was a rotten smell."

"It was an earthquake," Sebastien told him. "Two, actually, plus several smaller quakes."

"Earthquake? Well, I'll be..."

"You're welcome to join my crew, or we can drop you off at the nearest town. We should be coming up on Little Prairie soon."

The man looked about uncertainly. "I've always done flats, never a keel."

"Not much different, heading downriver. You can leave us at New Orleans if you choose."

"Appreciate the offer, but think I'll get off at Little Prairie, make my way home. Hey, I'm from Kentucky. You don't think the earthquake did damage there, do ya?"

"It hit New Madrid hard," Sebastien said, "but no telling how far the damage spread."

"Only one person died," Tori added, "and her heart gave out." She suspected Kentucky had suffered damage. She knew church bells had rung on the East Coast, but she kept quiet about that. It seemed she had set the man's worries to rest, for after he got a bite to eat he took up a pole and, accepting some good-natured jeering from the keelers, set himself to learning how to propel a "real" boat.

As darkness neared, Sebastien decided they would tie up for the night. "Away from any high banks and on an island if possible," he reminded his crew, but Tori didn't think they needed the guidance. Tremors had continued throughout the day, some of them quite strong. Once again he gave the men the option of staying on board or sleeping on the ground. The man they had rescued, chose to go ashore, but almost everyone else stayed. Jenny headed to the cabin to get ready for bed, but gave Tori a look before departing. Tori guessed if she didn't join her chaperon soon, Jenny would come looking for her.

"Don't know how long this shaking will continue, but we should be through the worst of it," Sebastien said as he helped her down from the roof. He must have seen something in Tori's expression, for he added, "What? Have you had another dream?"

Tori bit down on her bottom lip. "No, but I don't think the danger is over. Look, the comet is still overhead."

He gave the comet a cursory glance. "Did you expect it to disappear overnight? It was visible for months before the earthquake and will probably still be around for months after. I'm still not convinced they're even related."

"Gravity."

"What?"

"You know, gravity. Isaac Newton? The apple falling from the tree?" She knew Isaac Newton had lived in the seventeenth century, but wasn't sure how well his work was known in the nineteenth.

"I know what gravity is, but I'm not sure what it has to do with earthquakes or comets."

"Simple. The gravity produced by the comet contributed to the stress in the earth responsible for the earthquake." Tori was making this up, but not from whole cloth. Shortly before she was born, a scientist had made a big fuss about the New Madrid fault, claiming another big quake was imminent due to the gravitational forces of the planets aligning. He had even predicted the day and time.

He'd been wrong, but it had revived interest in the fault and the series of massive earthquakes which had been nearly forgotten even by those who lived within the seismic zone. Having experienced the ferocity of the earthquakes, it seemed strange that people would have forgotten about them, but that's how people were. No one from this time was still alive in her time. Tori shivered. *No one, that is, but me.*

Sebastien cocked his head to one side. "You're very well-educated for a woman. Do all women on the East Coast attend school?"

Tori didn't know. "Not all, but if a family can afford it, why not?"

"My parents saw to it that I went to school, but argued about my sister. My father didn't think it was necessary for her to go."

"Who won?"

Sebastien smiled. "My mother."

Chapter 16

Despite delays due to blockages, they arrived at Little Prairie the next morning—or at least they arrived at where it had once stood. It was now covered by water.

"Are you sure this is the right spot?" Roger asked. "I barely recognize the river in many places."

"Look." Sebastien pointed to where a few roofs could be seen poking above the water. The odors of sulfur and methane, even worse than they had smelled at New Madrid, hung over the area.

"Where are the people?" Jenny asked.

"Made for higher ground, most like," said Roger.

"If they had time." Sebastien looked grim.

"We need to stop," said Tori.

"Why? There's nothing we can do."

"The lass is right. We should see if there are any survivors."

"We can't bring anyone else on board. We are near capacity."

Roger scratched his head. "We could leave them some supplies."

Sebastien's expression darkened. "I'm not running a charity."

"The damage here is worse than in New Madrid," Jenny said in disbelief.

Tori laid a hand on Sebastien's arm. She felt bad asking him to give away his cargo after he had already done so much for her, but knew that if they continued without stopping, this flooded village would haunt her. "It could be a matter of life or death for them. Shouldn't we at least stop and see if anyone survived?" She wondered why she'd never even heard of Little Prairie until yesterday. New

Madrid was relatively well known for being destroyed by the earthquakes, but this small town must have been lost to history.

"Put in," Sebastien yelled to his men and then disappeared into the cabin area. Roger directed the crew as they tried to find a place to tie up. Most of the town appeared to be under water. The few houses that were not flooded had fallen down.

Once they were safely moored, a group including Sebastien, Roger, Tori, and Jenny, left the boat and began searching the rubble.

"Hallo! Anyone there?"

Tori was about ready to give up when they heard someone call out.

"Over here!" The voice came from one of the tumbledown houses. They approached it and stepped inside. One wall had collapsed and the structure looked like it might fall down at any moment. An elderly black man sat on the floor, his back propped up against the wall. His face fell when he saw their group. "I thought they done come back for me."

"Where did they go?"

"Master said they be headed west. The earth—it shook and cracked. Water done spewed out. Sand and mud, too. A big ol' hole formed in the middle of town. The houses, they sank, and black pus oozed up."

"Why didn't you go with them?" Roger asked.

"I'm too old, and I had to stay with Miz Metz."

"There's someone else here?" Jenny asked.

"My mistress. She's expecting and couldn't go neither."

Tori glanced around the room. "Where is she?"

"Upstairs."

Roger's brows shot up toward his receding hairline. "The next shake will reduce this place to rubble. What's she doing upstairs?"

"Not my place to tell Miz Metz what to do," the old man said.

Roger leveled a look at Sebastien.

"I'll go get her." He trudged up the stairs, pausing at every ominous creak. Tori held her breath until he disappeared from view.

A few minutes later he returned, carrying a dark-haired pregnant woman. He set her down when he reached the ground floor.

"They just left us." Her eyes were red and her face puffy. "Even my husband!"

"Don't 'spect they had much choice. The water came up powerful fast."

"It was good of you to stay, Zack, but don't you be making excuses for Jace. That man's going to get a piece of my mind if I ever lay eyes on his no-good self again."

"Do we take them on board or help them get to the others?" Roger asked.

"Can't take them on board. We've got no room and no way to care for Mrs. Metz." Sebastien turned his attention to Zack. "Do you know how far they went?"

"They sent out a scout. He waded 'bout a mile before 'e turn back for the others."

"Farther than a mile, then." Sebastien looked grim.

"We have to take them on board," Tori said. "They'd never make it."

"Did they have a destination in mind other than high ground?"

"Jace told me they would come back when the water went down, but if anything, the water has gotten deeper."

"What did they intend to do if the water didn't recede?" Sebastien asked.

"Head for New Madrid," Zack supplied.

"Jace never told me that! What were we supposed to do? He left us here to die."

"You know he left some food, Miz Metz. And he left me to care for you."

Tori's opinion of Mr. Metz was dropping by the minute. "We can make room. Mrs. Metz will stay with me and Jenny in your cabin and Zack will bunk with the men."

> 133

"Don't see we have much choice," Roger said, but he didn't look much happier than Sebastien.

"The men won't stand for having a pregnant woman aboard."

"You claimed they wouldn't accept me, but they got used to me."

"You don't understand."

"Then explain it to me."

Roger and Sebastien exchanged a look. "Why don't Jenny and I get these two something to eat from their supplies while you go get the boat ready," Roger suggested.

"We're not going back to New Madrid. We've already lost too much time."

"We'll take them to New Orleans or Natchez."

Sebastien stalked out of the room, leaving Tori to follow. She had to run to catch up. "Hey, I thought you were going to talk to me."

Sebastien slowed. He steered her toward the ruins of a house which at least gave them some shelter from the wind. "I told you about my sister."

"Your father didn't want her to go to school."

"After my mother died, my father remarried. I never liked my stepmother, but I was nearly grown by then and my father and I were gone as much as we were home, taking pelts and then transporting them down river. She took care of Ari and made my father happy. I ignored her as much as possible."

The weak sunlight did little to warm them, and tinted the world sepia. Tori stared out at the bleak sight of houses flooded to their roofs. Others appeared to have vanished altogether. It was a distressing sight and she knew Sebastien's story was not going to end any better.

"Then my father died." Sebastien, who had been standing against the wall, pushed himself away and began pacing. "The house should have been mine, but he left it to her."

"Your stepmother?"

"Yes." He stopped and stared at her, his eyes hard and angry. "Did he think I would throw her out in the street? He should have known I would never do such a thing."

"I'm sure he knew that, but he might have wanted her to have some security. She was his wife."

"I moved out, but left Ari there. As I said before, I wasn't around much."

"That seems sensible."

"I came back from a season of trapping to find her pregnant. Some cad had seduced and abandoned her. I wanted to kill him, but he'd gone back East."

Tori thought of her mother, abandoned by her father when Tori was a toddler.

"Martha, my stepmother, called her a whore. Said she wouldn't allow Ari to live with her once the baby was born." He clenched his hands into fists. "I should have found a place for her to stay, but I took her with me. I dragged my sister, a pregnant woman, down the river."

"What happened?" Tori asked, although she guessed. Childbirth was dangerous in the nineteenth century. The food she would have eaten on the *Fury* wouldn't have been very nourishing. She would have had no doctor, no sanitation.

"She went into labor early. We were far from any town. I tied up on the bank and took her to a nearby cave. I thought she might be more comfortable there, but things went badly. I didn't know what to do, so I finally went to see if I could find help."

After a moment of silence, Tori asked, "Did you?"

"No. I came back alone. There was a lot of blood, but my sister... she had disappeared."

"Disappeared?" It wasn't what she had expected him to say. "Where could she have gone?"

He shook his head. "It was raining, so not good tracking weather, and dark, by then. But she was bleeding. She headed toward the river, but the trail ended there. She must have fallen in or been taken by someone in a boat. Could have been Indians. More than likely, she drowned."

"You're afraid that if you take Mrs. Metz on board, she'll also die?"

Sebastien shrugged.

"Don't you think her chances of dying are greater if you leave her here?"

"I suppose, but it makes me uneasy. Come on. We'd best get out to the *Fury* and make arrangements."

Tori nodded and allowed Sebastien to help her on board. She felt her first stab of misgiving when they entered the tiny cabin that she'd come to think of as her new home. She had given Jenny the cot and now slept on a pallet on the floor.

"There's only one bed. Guess Jenny and Mrs. Metz can arm wrestle for it."

Tori smiled. She'd spent enough time with the keelers to know that was one of their favorite ways of settling disputes. "Mrs. Metz will get the bed. She's expecting. Jenny will join me on the floor." As uncomfortable as the bed was, she didn't think a great sacrifice.

"Zack's too old to be of much use. The men might resent him, especially since he's a slave."

Tori had wondered about that. "They'll listen to you," she said, hoping she spoke the truth. The crew was fiercely independent, but usually good about taking orders from the boss.

"I'll send some of them to help Roger and Jenny. The sooner we move on, the better."

Tori didn't disagree, but she wondered what else awaited them. She'd thought the worst of the damage occurred at New Madrid, but Little Prairie had been utterly destroyed. And she was the only one who knew that Sunday night's quake and aftershocks had only been the first of a series of three massive quakes. The worst was still to come.

* * *

Once the new refugees were aboard, they continued downriver. Within days, Tori conceded that Sebastien had been right. Mrs. Metz proved to be a difficult passenger. But of course they couldn't have left her.

Still, she found herself annoyed when the woman complained about the hardtack, corn mush, and coffee that comprised most of their meals. Sometimes Sebastien opened barrels of dried apples or peaches, but with river hazards amplified by floating wrecks, debris and new channels, he needed all hands on deck to steer the boat. No one was allowed to go hunting to supplement their food supply.

Zack borrowed a fishing line from one of the men and caught a few fish, which Roger fried up on the stove, but Mrs. Metz refused more than a bite, claiming the smell made her ill. Tori had never been fond of fish either, but Roger was a decent cook and she enjoyed the variety it offered.

Mrs. Metz confided to Tori and Jenny that her given name was Esme, but grew offended when Tori addressed her as such. "I'm Mrs. Metz to you, Miss Foster," she said.

Tori referred to her by her married name, but grew irritated with the woman's continued coolness to her. After all, Tori had been instrumental in convincing Sebastien to bring her along. The least Esme could do was be polite.

She said as much to Jenny one day as they knelt on the deck, washing out some of their clothes by the heat of a brazier.

"Perhaps we should have left her to her fate in Little Prairie."

Tori wasn't sure if the older woman was serious. "I just think she should show *some* gratitude." Tori still felt grateful that Sebastien had pulled her from the freezing water, and tried to remind herself of this whenever the realities of nineteenth-century living started to bring her down.

Jenny sighed. "Sometimes you seem quite sheltered for your age. I guess it comes of being brought up in the East rather than on the frontier. I used to be naive as well."

"I don't understand."

'Mrs. Metz thinks you're Sebastien's mistress."

Tori froze. She and Sebastien were not lovers. They'd shared no more than a few passionate kisses—not that it was any of Mrs. Metz's business anyway. She reminded herself that she was living in a judgmental time, when a woman's virginity was her most prized possession.

"I'm sorry, Victoria, but what did you expect people to think when you were traveling without a chaperon? Sebastien should never have agreed to take you on as a passenger, no matter what pressure you applied."

"Is that what you think? You've never treated me poorly."

"I try not to judge, but Eli wasn't sure about taking you in. In the end, though, he accepted Sebastien's money and kept his mouth shut, but you must have sensed his coolness toward you."

"I thought that was just his personality," Tori muttered, hoping she wasn't offending Jenny. "Is that why he wouldn't take my advice about leaving the house on the night of the quake?"

"Eli doesn't take orders from women, even virtuous ones. He's a dour fellow on the best of days."

"Then why did you marry him?" The question had bothered Tori for a while.

"My parents thought he was a good match. I didn't argue. He is a good provider, but I never expected him to move the family out of Kentucky. He's grown more intolerant since the move."

Tori hated that a kind woman like Jenny had married a man like Eli because she had so few choices. What would happen to her if she couldn't get the stone to work? She sat back on her haunches and hugged her knees. "If my reputation is already destroyed, why do I need you to chaperon me?"

"Not everyone out west is so unforgiving, but it's best that as few people as possible know about the time you spent on board without other women to watch over you."

"It's none of their business what I do or don't do."

"It's the way of the world."

Not in my time. But was that strictly true? People still pried into other people's lives, weighed their actions and found them wanting.

"Your mother should have explained all this to you."

"She died a couple of years ago."

"Is that when you took up theater work? Have you no relatives back East to contact? I worry we'll never find the boat you fell from."

"There's no one." Struck by the thought that even if she could send a note to the future, there really was almost no one who cared about her, Tori hugged her legs tighter. No one but Anne, and the few friends from high school and college she still kept in contact with.

"Have you given thought to what you'll do if we can't find the boat? Or if it didn't survive the earthquake?"

Since the boat was a fiction, Tori hadn't worried about its possible demise in the earthquake, but she'd been in the past for nearly two weeks now, and the necklace showed no signs of life. What if she truly was stuck here? "I don't want to consider that possibility, but if we reach New Orleans without finding them, Sebastien has agreed to take me to St. Louis." *And what then?* Becoming a teacher seemed her best bet.

Jenny wrung out her last garment. "He's a good man. He'll see you settled."

"What about Mrs. Metz and Zack? How will they get home?"

"Mr. Metz will have to send money for them to take passage to New Madrid."

"And if he doesn't?" She didn't have a lot of faith in a man who abandoned his pregnant wife, although now that she knew Esme better, she sympathized with him. "How will he know where to send the money? If he returns to Little Prairie, he'll find it deserted."

"Mrs. Metz can send a letter to New Madrid. If that doesn't work, she could sell Zack. She wouldn't get much for him, since he's elderly, but it should be enough to pay for a trip upriver."

Tori shivered. Buying and selling people seemed so wrong to her. "I don't understand how people tolerate slavery."

"Eli would never allow us to own slaves, even if we could have afforded it, but my parents kept a few house servants."

Tori shook her head. She would never have expected to agree with Eli about anything.

Sebastien walked up to them and gave her his now-familiar quizzical look. "You have a lot of strange notions. Slavery has always been around and probably always will be."

Unfortunately, he's right. "Lots of people are opposed to slavery. My parents were abolitionists."

"Well, you'd best keep that to yourself, especially as we travel farther south. They don't approve of foreigners meddling in their business."

At times like these she did feel like a foreigner. After hanging up her few clothes to dry, she excused herself and made her way to the cabin she shared with Mrs. Metz and Jenny. Relieved that Esme wasn't there, Tori plopped down on the pile of blankets that made up her bed and pulled the necklace from under her shirt. The beautiful blue stone seemed to mock her as she rubbed it, trying to bring it to life. The stone was warm from the heat of her body, but it didn't glow. Giving up once again, she tucked the necklace away. There had been no thunderstorms since her arrival in the nineteenth century, and she still held out some hope that lightning had played an integral part in her journey. But it was still December and it seemed unlikely there would be any thunderstorms until spring—a few months after the third, and last, violent quake.

Had she been brought here for a reason? She supposed she was in some way responsible for saving the lives of Mrs. Metz and Zack, although she suspected Jenny and Roger would have persuaded

Sebastien to do what was right even without her help. Her attempt to warn Sebastien of the upcoming disaster had gone so poorly, she hadn't even tried to warn anyone else. She'd been afraid to.

Pushing aside her melancholy thoughts, Tori tried to consider the positive. She was extremely well-educated for the time, probably better educated than most men. She had knowledge of the future. But when she set these perks alongside the drawbacks—the primitive state of medicine; the lack of rights for women; the acceptance—by most of the population—of slavery; and the fact that Coca-Cola wouldn't even be invented for almost a century—she felt she'd been dealt a losing hand. She had made some good friends here in the past. Jenny reminded her in many ways of both her mother, whom she still dearly missed, and Anne, who was now lost to her as well. But if she were to be honest, the most appealing part of the past was Sebastien. Why weren't there men like him in the twenty-first century?

Chapter 17

Since taking on Jenny, Sebastien saw much less of Victoria. She spent most of her time with the older woman and only sat with him when Jenny was present. He found himself missing her company more than he would have expected. With the arrival of Mrs. Metz, the other two women seemed to find the rooftop more appealing and to encourage them to continue coming, Sebastien brought them warm bricks for their hands and made a greater effort at conversation. Victoria didn't seem to mind silence, however. She seemed to find the view endlessly fascinating, which was strange since they passed little but trees. In so many ways she was unlike any other woman he had ever met.

He and his men had adjusted as best they could to the new hazards of the river. The area continued to be rocked by aftershocks, but on the water they were barely noticeable and grew even less so the farther the *Fury* continued downstream. On Christmas Eve they came upon another keelboat stuck on a sandbar. It was the *Revenge*.

"Ahoy there," Bob Rivers cried out as soon as they came within sight. "Can you give us a hand?"

The moment he saw the stalled boat, Sebastien had immediately shouted directions to his crew to try and avoid whatever dangerous currents might have led to the boat's grounding. By the time the *Fury* was safely anchored to shore, the boats were close enough that they recognized one another, and Sebastien left his keelboat to meet with Rivers. Rivermen regularly provided assistance to one another, and as Sebastien and the Rattler had partnered together for the descent, he was honor-bound to help.

"We feared you had perished in the earthquake," Sebastien said as he stepped onto the *Revenge*.

"We thought the same of you."

"Well, lucky for you, we've come to save your hide."

"We've already lost a full day." Rivers ran a hand through his close-cropped hair. Usually well-groomed for a riverman, he looked scruffy and haggard. "Damn river's completely changed. My guidebook is useless."

"Best to never rely too heavily on guidebooks. The Mississippi is like a living thing. Never stays the same for long."

"Can you get us free?"

Sebastien studied the other man. "I'll have to take a look."

"Then do so. Every day we lose is costing us money. What took you so long to get here anyway? We left New Madrid at the same time."

"And I went back to get my men and my passenger. I take it you did not?"

"What would be the point? I can always take on more crew in New Orleans. Now, I might have considered returning for the lovely Miss Foster."

"We've also picked up three victims of the quakes—a man who survived the wreck of his flatboat and a pregnant woman and her slave who were abandoned in Little Prairie."

"You're losing your edge, La Roche. Some people hailed us as we passed Little Prairie as well, but we kept on going."

"And yet here you are."

Rivers' brows drew together. "Just get me off this sandbar."

Sebastien examined the situation. Rivers and his crew had already tried pushing it off, of course, but they hadn't been able to budge it. He thought they might be able to lever it out with handspikes, but it might be faster if they could hire a team to pull them off.

"Have you gone ashore looking for help?" he asked Rivers.

"No. Why would I need to? I have your men now."

"We can try wiggling it out, but horses might be faster. It will cost you a bit, but time is money."

"Let's put the men to work. Horses will be a last resort."

Sebastien returned to the *Fury* where he put a team of men, under Roger's direction, to trying to free the *Revenge*. Then he went in search of Victoria, Jenny and Mrs. Metz. He found them by the stove.

"What's going on?" the pregnant woman asked the moment she saw him. "Why have we stopped? I need to get to New Orleans as soon as possible."

"We are partnered with the *Revenge*. The earthquake separated us, but now that we are back together, we have to help them out."

"How long will it take?"

"A few hours—if we're lucky."

"A few hours!" Mrs. Metz wailed.

"Calm yourself, Esme," Jenny said. "We've been fortunate not to get stranded on a sandbar ourselves."

"It's a hazard of river travel," Sebastien agreed.

"We could go ashore," Tori said. "I think we would all feel better if we spent some time on land."

"And risk being taken by Indians?" the pregnant woman asked.

Victoria's face fell. "Do you think we would be safe?" she asked Sebastien. "We would stay close to the river."

"I have another idea. Since it's Christmas Eve, we should see if a nearby homestead would be willing to host us for the holiday—for a fee, of course. It's possible Mrs. Metz might be able to stay there and be spared the rest of the river journey."

The women brightened at the prospect. "I would dearly love to get off this boat," Mrs. Metz said. "But why would they allow me to stay?"

"You must tell them your husband will reimburse them for your room and board."

"Send out the search party," Mrs. Metz said.

"I will accompany them myself," Sebastien said and went off to consult with the *Revenge*.

Rivers, of course, opposed the idea. "Give the men an extra ration of whiskey on Christmas and they'll be happy enough."

"That may be, but I think we could all do with a rest."

"Do as you please, but I'll be heading down river as soon as we get free. Taking on passengers has made you soft, La Roche. From what I hear, there was a time when you wouldn't let anything get in the way of a quick, profitable trip down river."

Sebastien clenched a fist, then deliberately released it. "I got into this business to make money. Seemed to me it was getting harder to make a decent living by trapping and trading. I make no apologies for that."

"Then why the sudden need to pamper your men? Or is it the women you want to indulge? Perhaps one woman in particular? The lovely Miss Foster? I might not mind prolonging my trip either if I was snuggled up with her."

Sebastien stepped closer to the other man. Rivers was taller, but Sebastien outweighed him and carried no extra flab. "You'll keep a civil tongue in your head about Miss Foster. Mrs. Sellers has come aboard as her chaperon."

"And if I don't? What will you do? Challenge me to a duel?"

Sebastien smiled. "Gentlemen duel. River men will stick a knife in your ribs while you're sleeping."

Rivers' eyes narrowed. "Never threaten me again. You don't know who you're dealing with."

"A rattlesnake? Bob Rivers? You and your boat came out of no where a couple years ago, although you've done well for an Easterner."

"For an Easterner? I've built up a business as profitable as yours in half the time."

Sebastien inclined his head. Rivers was a successful patron, Easterner or no. But he had started with money, an advantage Sebastien lacked. "My men will help get you off this sand bar and then you can stay or go as you please. But if you speak disrespectfully of Miss Foster again, I will pummel you into a pulp."

Rivers held up his hands in surrender, though his eyes were still hard as flint. "So that's the way of it? You've fallen for her. Well, take my word, she's not who she says she is."

Sebastien left without comment, but he knew deep inside that Rivers was right. Victoria was lying to him.

* * *

It took only an hour of hacking through the thick undergrowth and trees felled by the earthquakes to reach a house lit by lanterns and a bonfire. As soon as the mouthwatering aroma of a roast pig reached Sebastien and the two men he had brought with him, their spirits rose and they approached the homestead cautiously, but with hope.

A barrel-chested man answered their knock on the door and invited them into a room warmed by a fire and burning candles. Two women, one white and one black, sat on the sofa doing needlework while a handful of children played by the hearth.

"What brings you three out on such a cold night?" the man asked, after introducing himself as Max Legrand.

"I've two keelboats I'm taking down river. One is currently stuck and seeing that it's Christmas, my passengers and crew would like to join you for the holiday. We have good Kentucky whiskey to trade, or coin, if you prefer."

"We have a large pig roasting, enough for paying guests, no?" he asked his wife.

The white woman nodded without looking up from her work.

"We have a pregnant woman aboard that we rescued from the flooding upriver. I'd appreciate a warm bed for her and my other two female passengers. It can get mighty cold on the river."

This time the woman looked up, her forehead creased with worry. "They can stay in the barn."

"It is Christmas, my dear," her husband reminded her. "Would you have this woman, with child, just as Mary was, stay in the stables?"

She didn't flinch. "We have our own children to think about."

"They can stay in the back room and Lucy will tend them. You will not be bothered, Monique."

His wife did not look pleased, but she bent her head to her work without further argument. The black woman rose and said she would prepare the room.

"Let's have a drink and reach an agreement," Max said. He led the men out to the fire where he poured them some home brew.

Sebastien spent the next half hour haggling with Max, but in the end he got the supplies he needed, warm beds for the women, and a celebration for the men. They returned to the boat where Roger put the men on rotation so that all would have a chance to enjoy the party, but the boat would never be left unattended. Before any of the men could leave, however, they had to free the *Revenge*.

Zack, Mrs. Metz's slave, and Sebastien helped the women to shore. The return trip to the Legrand farm was easier since they had already cleared a path, but Mrs. Metz was unable to move quickly. Eventually, Sebastien handed his barrel of whiskey off to Zack, then draped her arm around his neck and, supporting most of her weight, half-carried her to the house. By the time they arrived, all five were winded, but Lucy had made up three pallets on the floor and was brewing a hot toddy. "My mother taught me how to make this. It will warm you up."

"I would love to try your recipe," Victoria said.

Mrs. Metz looked doubtful. "After all that walking, I'm not cold."

"Well, I am," Jenny said.

Lucy didn't appear to take offense at Mrs. Metz's words. She poured cups for Sebastien, Jenny, and Victoria. He took a sip and found it had a pleasant fruity taste. "I will see you tomorrow at the party, ladies," Sebastien said. Still annoyed from his altercation with

Rivers, he wasn't feeling particularly festive, but the whole point of going ashore had been so everyone, himself included, could get a break from the harsh conditions of life on the boat.

Victoria took his arm and gave it a squeeze. "I think this just might be the strangest Christmas I've ever had, but it's also one of the most memorable."

As Sebastien glanced down into her eyes, he had to agree. He would never forget this strange and dangerous trip down river—not the near-constant shaking of the ground, the destruction of towns, the alteration of the river, or the unusual woman he had pulled from its depths.

He had the feeling his life would never be the same again.

Chapter 18

A dusting of snow fell overnight and the women awoke to a white Christmas. The Legrands had other servants—or perhaps slaves; Tori wasn't certain—besides Lucy, and tables had been set up in the barn for the party. It wasn't where they kept the animals. The house was built upon a rise and the cows and horses were kept in what she thought of as a walk-out basement, under the main house to make the best use of body heat. The building where the party was held was used to store equipment and the harvest. Bags of grain had been pushed to the edges of the walls, and plows and other large implements temporarily moved outside. The floor had been swept clean and a fire kindled in a makeshift brazier. Sebastien had brought the first keg of whiskey and although the pig was still roasting, other dishes had been set up. The sight and smell of baked beans, fresh bread and butter, potatoes, and apple pie made Tori realize how hungry she was. To her surprise, on one corner of the table sat a pitcher of eggnog, which Max proceeded to liberally spike with Sebastien's whiskey.

The family, consisting of the parents and five children varying in age from toddler to teen, joined her, Sebastien and Mrs. Metz. After serving the food, the servants helped themselves, taking their plates to another table. Tori saw Zack eating there as well. She had just helped herself to a piece of pie, along with yet another serving of eggnog, when Rat arrived.

"Bob Rivers," he said, extending his hand to Max. "Captain of the *Revenge*. Good of you to share your meal with us."

Tori almost choked on her pie. Apparently the Rattler could be charming when it suited him.

"My pleasure," Max replied, beaming. "We don't get many visitors. You must tell me the news. Have you felt the earthquakes? Our house is fine, but some of my neighbors suffered damage. And they still come! Every day the ground shakes."

"They were worse up stream. Mrs. Metz is from Little Prairie. The entire town was destroyed."

"Everyone left, including my husband," Mrs. Metz said. "Only Zack stayed with me." She dabbed at her eyes with a napkin.

"That's dreadful. How could a man abandon his pregnant wife?" Even Monique seemed shaken out of her complacency.

"Water came out of the ground, black filthy stuff. The land sank until the river overran it. Whole buildings disappeared. None of the houses were unscathed, but they left us in the house farthest from the flooding. If Captain La Roche hadn't rescued us—well, I don't know what would have happened."

"Where did the townsfolk go?" Max asked.

"Higher ground," Mrs. Metz said vaguely.

"Zack told us they were headed to New Madrid, but that's where I live. The town sustained considerable damage, although no flooding," Jenny said. "The residents are temporarily living in a tent city."

"How far apart are the two settlements? Do you think they could have made it in this cold?"

"Twenty miles or more," Sebastien said. "It would not be an easy journey. Not only would they have to battle the cold, but the damage done to the land as well—fissures, cracks, and fallen trees."

"Your husband might be dead," Monique said. "Leaving you behind was a blessing."

"If there was any way to survive, I'm sure Jace found it." Mrs. Metz didn't seem overly concerned about her husband's fate, but Tori couldn't really blame her after the man's actions. Sebastien would never have left her, had they been in the Metzes' situation. Other men she had known, such as Ned, might have behaved as poorly as Mr. Metz.

Sebastien and Bob Rivers kept the Legrands entertained with stories about life on the river and the news they had heard while in St. Louis.

The Legrands described the frightening appearance of a steamboat along the Mississippi just days earlier. "You should have seen it," Max said. "It puffed and bellowed like a hog, and the owner claimed it could travel upriver nearly as fast as it could go down."

Sebastien and Bob exchanged glances. "If that's true, it could spell the death of the keelboat industry," Sebastien said.

Bob shook his head. "Steamboats regularly travel the rivers out East, but I didn't think they could handle a river as wild as the Mississippi."

"This one seemed to be doing all right. Survived the earthquakes and everything."

Monique smirked. "I for one would like to see the river tamed. It might bring civilization to the valley."

Tori thought her words rather rude, considering the company.

"It will just bring more Americans, my dear," Max said, his round face growing more red as he continued to eat and drink. "Civilization fled the area the day the United States bought Louisiana."

"Speaking of the United States," Jenny said. "Do you think they'll declare war on England? And if they do, will there be much fighting here on the frontier?"

"The Indians will side with the Redcoats and scalp us in our beds," Monique said.

"It won't come to war," Max predicted. "The United States won't want to take on the might of Great Britain again."

"I hope you are right," Jenny said.

Tori kept her mouth shut.

Rivers snorted. "They'll have little choice but to declare war if Britain keeps harassing our ships and impounding our men into the

British Navy. But I don't think it will matter much in the West unless they capture the port of New Orleans. That would put the likes of us rivermen out of business and leave farmers such as yourself with no where to sell your crops."

Tori knew that war was inevitable, but since she recalled that the Battle of New Orleans had been won by the Americans and fought after the official close of the war, she didn't think the city had ever fallen into enemy hands. Still, she realized she really didn't know how the war had affected the lives of people on the frontier.

The mood, which had been darkening, lifted when the first group of men from the keelboats arrived. They had dug a trench and managed to get enough water under the *Revenge* to haul her free. Rivers visibly relaxed, now that he knew his boat was safe, but he didn't insist on an immediate departure, as Tori had feared from what Sebastien had told her. He probably realized the men would mutiny if he kept them from their Christmas dinner.

"Pig's done!" one of the servants called and a cheer went up from the crowd. He brought in the roasted animal and other servants assisted him in slicing it up. A handful of neighbors from less prosperous homesteads arrived and the whiskey flowed freely. Once everyone had eaten their fill, the guests brought out an assortment of instruments, including a violin that had seen better days. The owners of the instruments gathered in the corner and began to scratch out a tune. Others pushed some of the tables as far out of the way as possible and began to dance.

"Shall we?" Sebastien asked with a smile.

Tori remembered how they had danced together at New Madrid the night before the quakes struck. His life had been turned upside down since then, but hers had already been crazy. She glanced over at the makeshift dance floor. The steps looked similar to the ones from the dance in New Madrid, but less formal, the difference between a weekly event and something that probably only happened once or twice a year. She didn't think she would make too much of a fool of herself and, frankly, she had drunk enough whiskey not to care. She returned Sebastien's smile and offered him her hand.

He led her onto the floor, where no one seemed to mind them joining a set already in progress. Jenny danced with Roger and Max partnered his wife. Thanks to the riverboat men, there was once again a surplus of male dancers and Tori found herself passed from one partner to another until she was exhausted. Apologizing to her last partner, she left the dance floor, helped herself to anther glass of eggnog, lit a candle from the lantern, and slipped back to the house. Jenny was still going strong, but Mrs. Metz had already retired for the night. Tori wasn't quite ready for bed, so she entered the off-shoot of the house where the animals lived. She wandered over to a brown horse with gentle eyes and patted it on the neck. The horse nickered and nuzzled her.

"She wants a treat."

Tori looked over in surprise. She hadn't realized anyone else was there. Sebastien leaned against the door of the last stall, nearly blending into the darkness. "I didn't think to bring any food."

"You were the belle of the ball."

Tori laughed. "Not hard when belles are in such short supply."

He stepped closer and cupped her chin. "Are you for bed, then?"

Tori swallowed. "It'll be nice to have a warm place to sleep tonight." *Even if I am still on the floor.* "Are you heading back to the *Fury*?"

"Soon." He caressed her cheek. "Last time we danced you tried to warn me about the earthquake. I wouldn't listen. Have you any predictions tonight?"

"I told you there would be more quakes."

"I could have predicted that. A large earthquake always produces tremors."

"Big quakes. We're not yet done with them."

"And how do you know that? Did you ask the horse?"

Tori sighed. She was so sick of lying. "I could tell you the truth, but you would never believe me."

"Try me."

She pulled away from his hold and sank down onto the floor, setting her candle carefully to one side. After a moment, he did the same and they sat with their backs against the stall door, the earthy smell of animals surrounding them. "I'm not from here."

"No, you're from back East."

"That's not entirely true, although I have visited there."

Sebastien didn't appear surprised. "Europe? You speak differently than anyone I've ever heard."

"No. I've never been to Europe. I'm from St. Louis, just as you are."

"It's a big town for this far west, but I still think I would have seen you sometime if you've lived there all your life."

"It's been my home except for the years I spent away at college."

Now she'd managed to surprise him. "College? It's very rare for a woman to go to college."

"Not in my time."

"Your time?"

"When I said I wasn't from here, I really should have said I'm not from *now*. I'm from the future, Sebastien. That's how I knew about the earthquakes and how I know that the United States will go to war with Britain. It'll happen sometime next year."

"Victoria, we have both had more than enough to drink tonight, but do you really expect me to believe such an outlandish tale? We are born, we live, and we die. That's all."

"I was born in 1990, Sebastien. I have seen things you cannot even imagine." He didn't move, but she could sense him withdrawing from her.

"Tell me of them."

"I'm not sure how much is safe to share. Knowledge of the future can be dangerous. But New Madrid will be destroyed during the third big quake."

"We have already had at least two 'big' quakes."

"I know, but I'm counting all the quakes that happened that first day as one. There will be another big quake in January and a third in February. I wish I could remember the exact dates, but I didn't know I'd be traveling back in time and so I wasn't able to prepare."

He was quiet for a while. His arm, already rock solid, had tightened next to hers, yet he didn't move away. "You are strange in many ways, but how is such a thing possible?"

"I don't know, but it has something to do with my necklace." She pulled it over her head and ran her finger along the smooth facets. The blue stone remained cool to the touch, the crystal beautiful, but unresponsive.

Sebastien reached for it. "May I?"

She handed it over, fighting anxiety as the portal to her old life left her possession. She trusted Sebastien, didn't she? She wouldn't have broken down and told him the truth if she had any doubts.

He rolled the pendant between his fingers. "I know little about jewelry, but although I can see how this piece might be valuable, I don't see how it could bring you to the past."

"It was late and snowing. Mr. Henderson—" she felt Sebastien stiffen and knew he had not forgotten her words about the man who seemed determined to ruin her life. "He confronted me after the reception." She heard a sound from the far end of the stable where it attached to the house.

Sebastien heard it as well. He motioned for her to be silent and sprang to his feet. He moved silently down the length of the stalls, his dark evening clothes blending into the night. She heard the faintest whisper of sound as he climbed the stairs. After a few moments, he returned to the circle of light provided by her candle. "I didn't see anyone. Whoever it was is gone. Probably one of the men mistaking their way in the dark after too much whiskey."

"Could be," Tori agreed, but she felt uneasy. She didn't trust anyone but Sebastien with the truth. There was power in knowledge and others might try to force her to tell them what she knew of the future—if they didn't just want to burn her for a witch.

Sebastien handed the necklace back. "You never intended to give me this, did you?"

She ducked her head. "No. I'm sorry, but it's my only way to get home."

"Have you tried to go home?"

"Of course, but I don't know how to get it to work."

"Perhaps there was only enough magic in the stone for a one-way trip."

The thought had crossed her mind, but Tori refused to give up hope of returning to her own time. "So you believe me?" She wasn't sure she would have believed him, if their situations were reversed.

"My mother claimed there was more to life than we could know. This angered my father, since it went against the teachings of the priests, even though he wasn't very religious."

It wasn't an answer, but it would have to do. "I'd better get to bed."

"Aye. Hangovers or no, I don't know how long I'll be able to keep the Rattler in port."

Chapter 19

As Sebastien had feared, Rivers was raring to go in the morning. He yelled and bullied his men, then cast off—leaving behind a man who had passed out at the Legrand place. Sebastien took a more leisurely approach, but still insisted that the holiday was over.

He went to get the women, but when he arrived at the farm, he found only Victoria, Jenny, and Rivers' bleary-eyed boatman waiting for him.

"Mrs. Metz and Zack have been invited to stay with the Legrands until the baby is born. Mrs. Metz and Mrs. Legrand have hit it off. Actually, she extended a half-hearted invitation to me as well, but since she knew I had no relatives willing to pay my board, I knew there would be strings attached. I want to remain here even less than I wanted to stay in Ste. Gen."

They set out for the boat, but Sebastien and Victoria fell behind the other two so they could speak privately. He hadn't slept much after returning to the boat with Victoria's strange tale rattling around in his brain.

The logical part of him couldn't accept it as true, but he fully believed that *she* believed it. She thought she had traveled more than two hundred years into the past, though perhaps she had only struck her head before or after falling into the river. He knew a man who had been perfectly normal until a beam had fallen on his head. Ever since that day, he'd acted like a child. Not that there was anything childlike about Victoria. "So, tell me more about the coming war. Will the United States prevail once more against Britain?"

She had that wary look on her face once more. "We will win, but I can't give you details."

That's convenient.

She seemed to read his skepticism. "How much could you tell me about life in 1611? Could you tell me who won which war and which battles?"

"I guess not."

"Plus, there's always the danger of changing the future if you change the past. That's what always happens in the movies."

"Moovees?"

"Movies are like plays." They stopped at a fallen tree and he helped her over it. "Say you go back in time and kill your own grandfather. Then you'll never be born."

"Then you had better not kill anyone."

"I don't plan to."

"What becomes of St. Louis?"

"It grows into a big city, but it's past its heyday by my time. Other cities have grown bigger and more important."

Sebastien digested her words. While it saddened him to hear his home would peak and decline over the next two hundred years, he understood enough about history to realize life was not static. There was always change. Her story made a crazy kind of sense, but was it true? With the exception of her coat, her clothes appeared normal. But the coat had always troubled him, made as it was of a strange material. And there was her strange behavior to consider. She was often quiet, but not meek. She looked him directly in the eyes and never acted subserviently. She spoke against slavery, and until Jenny came aboard, had not seemed overly concerned about her reputation. Could all this be because she had come from another time?

Most troubling of all, if she were telling the truth, then the necklace might be activated at any time. She could leave his life as suddenly as she had entered it.

* * *

Life resumed on the river. After returning to the *Fury*, Sebastien didn't ask her anything more about the future, although she felt his curious gaze on her at times. The river was still clogged with debris and they could still see trees shaking on land from time to time, but most tremors could not be felt on the boat beyond a gentle rocking, and the damage on land, visible from the river, lessened with each passing mile. Barring any complications, Sebastien thought they would reach New Orleans shortly after the new year.

"Tomorrow we should pass Island #99 where the pirates have a stronghold," Sebastien told Tori and Jenny, but to their surprise, when they reached that stretch of river, the island was gone and presumably the pirates as well.

Tori heard members of the crew muttering about divine justice, but she saw more than a few of them crossing themselves. She felt tempted to send up a quick prayer herself, even though she knew earthquakes and other natural disasters were just random events. Certainly the people of New Madrid and Little Prairie had done nothing to deserve the destruction of their towns.

On New Year's Eve, Sebastien asked her to play for the men again, and Dalton grudgingly let her use his fiddle. Sebastien also gave the men an extra ration of whiskey, and spirits were high. She played for a couple of hours and would have played longer if the men had their way, but she begged exhaustion and handed the fiddle back to Dalton. Playing had reminded her of her old life and she greeted the new year in a pensive frame of mind. She longed for the convenience of fast food and cell phones and thought she would never again take the luxury of central heating and electricity for granted. But not everything had been lost to her. She still had her music, and although she missed Anne, she had Jenny, Roger, and most of all, Sebastien. Her real life had begun to feel remote, as if it had been lived by someone else.

When they floated into New Orleans, the crew let out a cheer. Tori grabbed Sebastien's hand as the most populous city she had seen since leaving her own time, came into view. The harbor was full of boats of every description: flatboats, keelboats, sailboats, and even the steamboat the Legrands had told them about. Named for the city, the *New Orleans* had successfully completed her virgin voyage down the Ohio and Mississippi despite being caught up in the earthquakes.

"Civilization," Jenny whispered. "From here I can book passage to Virginia."

"Will you return to the frontier once the earthquakes abate?" Tori asked.

"I don't know. I suppose it is my duty to my husband and children, but I can't see going back to New Madrid. If Eli would move to St. Louis or even return to Kentucky, I might consider it."

A mist lay like a blanket upon the town, casting the pastels into shadow and masking the signs of peeling paint and weathered planks. The streets were laid out in a grid with houses clustered close to the riverfront. A few hundred feet from the river, at the end of an open square, stood the cathedral, an elegant brick building towering over most of the town. The houses were mostly made of wood, and some had verandas attached to the front or actually circling the entire building.

"It's charming," Tori said.

"Is that the best you can say?" Sebastien grumbled, but the twinkle in his eyes gave him away. "Have you been here before?"

"No."

"It looks much the same as the last time I saw it. I don't think the earthquakes did any damage here."

As they tied up at the dock, the cacophony of sound overwhelmed Tori's ears. The bustle of commerce, babble of multiple languages, and the croaking of bullfrogs bombarded senses grown used to the quiet of the river. Between the levee and the warehouses were hundreds of booths selling fish, fruit, vegetables, and trinkets.

"What happens now?" Tori asked, taken aback by the chaos.

"I'll be busy disposing of our cargo, but I'll have Roger escort you and Jenny to the hotel. The men will be anxious to visit the taverns and, um, such." He turned a bit red.

Brothels. Tori still found it amusing that Sebastien treated her as if she were innocent of such things, but after her experience with Ned back in her own time, she had no desire to take unnecessary risks in this time, when protections for women were almost nonexistent.

"How will I go about booking passage to Virginia?"

"Roger can help with that as well. And then he can show the two of you around, if you're interested."

"I would like that," Tori said. New Orleans was still known as a mystical city, full of voodoo and magic. She wondered if someone here could advise her how to activate the crystal necklace.

The men worked quickly to unload the cargo and move it in a warehouse Sebastien rented for that purpose. Soon they would be given part of their wages and leave to go raise a ruckus.

"May I take you to dinner tomorrow?" Sebastien asked Tori.

"Of course," she answered, recalling the last time she had been on a date, although she had not considered it such at the time. When Ned had insisted on picking up the check, she'd thought he was being kind since she was going through a tough time. Ned, however, had other ideas. She could barely even remember her last date before that. "I'll look forward to it."

They left the *Fury*, Sebastien going one way to meet with brokers interested in buying his products, and Roger taking Jenny and Tori to the hotel. An olive-skinned maid led the women to their room, where they dropped off their luggage and took a few minutes to freshen up. However, Roger was waiting, Tori was eager to explore, and Jenny was anxious to get the next stage in her journey settled, so they didn't linger. When they joined Roger a few minutes later in the lobby, he had also washed up and donned the jacket and breeches he had worn to the New Madrid dance and Christmas dinner.

He offered them each an arm, and they strolled out of the hotel and onto the street. Tori wondered whether any of the people who saw them thought Roger was her father. She felt a tug of loss for her own father, which she hadn't felt in years. Many of the children she had gone to school with had parents who were divorced, but at least they usually saw their dads on weekends and holidays. Eventually she had grown to accept her fatherless state and she had stopped wondering where he was and if he would ever return.

"I want to thank you and Sebastien for taking me on board. I don't know what I would have done if I hadn't been able to leave New Madrid."

Roger smiled. "It was our pleasure. Rescuing the two of you—and even the troublesome Mrs. Metz—has made a memorable journey even more so."

"Tori, I worry about what will happen to you. Your people must have perished on the river."

"They could be here in New Orleans."

Jenny looked doubtful. "If I have enough money to purchase two tickets, will you come with me to Virginia? My cousin will take us both in."

Tori was touched. She had known Jenny for less than a month. "I will always appreciate your kindness, but Sebastien has promised to see me settled in St. Louis if I can't find my touring group."

"You shouldn't travel on the *Fury* without a chaperon."

"Don't worry about Victoria. I will make sure no harm comes to her," Roger said. He and Jenny exchanged glances and Tori wondered, not for the first time, if there were something between them. Roger was nearly a decade older than Jenny and Jenny was still married, but hearts didn't always conform to propriety. However, in a time when divorce was rare, she supposed they could never be together, which saddened her.

As they walked back to the docks, they passed shops selling food and other everyday items. There were taverns already catering to a large and boisterous crowd despite the relatively early hour.

"We will search for passage first, then explore." They approached the oceangoing vessels, Roger easily communicating with the captains whether they spoke English, French, or Spanish. In less than an hour, he had found a place for Jenny on a ship sailing the next day.

Not having expected such quick results, Jenny asked to be taken back to the hotel so she could prepare. "You don't mind, do you?" she asked Tori. "Go ahead and let Roger show you the sights." She didn't seem to think Tori needed chaperoning around the older man.

"Where should we go?" Roger asked after they dropped Jenny off. "A dress shop? We won't be here long enough to have something custom-fitted, but you could purchase some fabric or they might have some ready-made. Sebastien wants you to have a dress for your dinner and authorized me to charge it to his account."

Tori would have loved to visit a dress shop. Though she was growing used to wearing long dresses, she was heartily sick of her charity clothes, which had never fit that well and were already well worn. "That sounds wonderful, but there's something I need to do first. I need to visit a magic shop. Some place selling potions, charms—that sort of thing."

Roger's eyes grew wide. "I'm aware of such shops, but I have never been in one. Are you sure that's where you want to go?"

"I could use some good luck," she said. It was true, but not the whole truth. However, she was unwilling to confide in any one other than Sebastien.

The furrows on Roger's brow cleared. "Why didn't I think of that? And maybe a love spell or two," he added with a wink. "Though I don't think a pretty girl like you needs such a thing to catch a man's eye." He pressed a handful of coins into her hand.

Again, Tori was overwhelmed by the kindness of her friends. "Thank you. I will try and repay you—"

"No need. It's a gift." He led her away from the river, onto streets where the houses were smaller and more closely crowded together. He stopped in front of a one-story building with a wide porch and an intriguing aroma of herbs and spices drifting from the interior.

Tori took a deep breath and pushed the door open. A woman with smooth brown skin stood behind the counter. She wore a simple long-sleeved gown with a colorful scarf twisted around her head. Hoop earrings with multi-colored charms hung from her ears. She inclined her head toward Tori, but said nothing.

Tori gave her a nervous smile and looked around the shop. Shelves covered the walls. One held jars filled with spices, while another housed skulls and dolls that reminded her of the Day of the Dead. Voodoo dolls, she guessed, but surely the skulls were fake. At least, she hoped so. Yet another shelf held potions and candles. Objects hung from the ceiling—it seemed as if every spare inch of space had been put to good use.

"Can I help you?" the woman asked after Tori had looked around.

Tori hesitated. Should she buy something? The coins Roger had given her weighted her pocket. The woman might be more willing to answer her questions if she made a sale, too. "Have you any love potions?" she asked, recalling Roger's teasing suggestion.

The woman studied her with dark eyes. "You cannot make someone fall in love with you. It is forbidden."

Well, duh. Tori didn't believe in spells, but she wouldn't have expected the owner of a magic shop to admit to such a thing. However, she knew aphrodisiacs existed and that was what she had expected to purchase. She didn't have much faith in them either, but thought she had read somewhere that science upheld some of their claims. "No love spells? Well, what about a good-luck charm?"

"I didn't say I had no love spells, only that it was impossible to force someone to fall in love with you."

"Then what does the spell do?"

The woman walked over to the shelf with the bottles and pulled one down. "This will strengthen the bond between lovers." She handed the bottle to Tori.

Tori held it up to the light. It was filled with some sort of liquid. The bottle itself was made of dark amber glass, so she couldn't be sure what color the fluid was, but it looked reddish. "What do I do with this?"

"Pour a few drops into the man's drink. Yours as well, if you wish."

"And it's safe?" Not that she could trust the word of a nineteenth-century voodoo priestess. The woman might well believe her wares were safe, but who knew what creepy ingredients made up the potion?

The woman smiled. "Love is not safe."

Well, she isn't wrong there. "How much?"

The woman told her a figure that meant nothing to her. Tori pulled out a few of the coins. Darn, she should have asked Roger what they were worth. "This is all I have." The remaining coins seemed to jingle in her pocket, although she knew they made no sound. "All I can afford," she amended.

"It is more than enough for the love potion. Enough to pay for your questions as well."

Tori felt the hair raise on the back of her neck. How on earth had the woman known she wanted to ask questions? A lucky guess? Or did she actually have some sort of power? Slowly she pulled the necklace over her head and set it on the counter alongside the bottle. "Have you ever seen something like this?"

The woman picked it up and studied it carefully. "Very fine work. Real silver."

Tori brushed that aside. "Do you know what this is? What it can do?"

The woman set the necklace back down. "I have heard tales."

Tori's heart leapt. "You have? Then you know how to make it work?"

She shook her head and ran her fingers along the stone again. "The power is drained. I do not know how to restore it."

Tori replaced the necklace with shaking fingers. She could go to someone else, but her chances of returning home seemed bleak. "I see."

The woman took one of the coins, but slid the other across the counter. "I am sorry I could not help you. But I will give you some advice. Magic comes at a price. Always. Even such as that." She gestured toward the love potion. "Use it with care."

Tori nodded, idly fingering the necklace beneath her dress. No worries; she had no intention of actually using the potion and didn't believe in magic.

Or did she?

Chapter 20

"She couldn't help me," Tori told Roger upon leaving the shop.

He glanced over at the bottle she carried, but kept his curiosity to himself. "There are other shops."

She was tempted, but also afraid. Something about this woman, with her melodious voice and uncanny intuition, had given her the creeps. She didn't think the woman meant her harm, but the atmosphere of the shop brought to mind dark forces and shook her modern belief that black magic didn't exist. Evil was real; she'd seen enough of that in both her own time and this one. Time travel was real. Why not spells, potions, and portents?

She took a deep breath and exhaled. "I think I've had enough of voodoo for the day. Perhaps we could go to a dress shop, like you suggested earlier." She wondered how much the coins he had given her were worth. Enough for a new dress?

Roger beamed. "I know just the place. You might not believe it to look at me now, but when I was younger I prided myself on my wardrobe and had an eye for the ladies as well." His pace quickened as he led her away from the voodoo shop. He didn't return to the elegant, well-spaced shops near the river; those, Tori guessed, would be too expensive. He stopped in front of a rather modest building with a deep front porch. He opened the door with a flourish and held it so she could enter before him.

It took a moment for her eyes to adjust to the shadowed interior, but once they did, she saw that the building was larger than she had thought, being long and skinny. Like the voodoo shop, this store made the most of every inch of space, with shelves crammed with bolts of material and worktables overflowing with partially completed garments. A small army of women sat at the worktables plying their needles.

"Roger?" A short, round woman walked from the back of the store, a smile creasing her face. "It's been a long time since I've seen you." As she got closer, her gaze zeroed in on Tori. "You devil, still picking the prettiest girls around."

Tori blushed. The woman had probably already guessed her dress size and was contemplating how much money she could squeeze out of Roger.

Roger laughed. "Dora, you flatter me. This lovely lady belongs to Sebastien."

Tori felt her hackles rise, but reminded herself of when she was.

"Sebastien, hmm?" The woman pursed her mouth. "Thought he usually held himself aloof."

"Pulled her out of the river."

Tori decided she'd had enough of being spoken about as if she weren't there. "I would like to see anything you have ready-made that might fit me."

"To be charged to Sebastien's account," Roger broke in.

Dora called one of her assistants over and spoke rapidly to her in French. The girl bowed to Tori and gestured for her to follow.

Tori slipped out of her coat and passed it to Roger. "Hold that for me, will you?" She didn't want the dressmaker to examine the fabric or see the zipper.

The girl showed her to a small fitting room and said something to her in French.

Tori had picked up a few words and phrases from constant exposure to the language, but she still could not speak it. "Do you speak English?"

"A little," the girl said with a heavy accent.

"I need something to wear to dinner tomorrow and would like to buy a day dress and some undergarments." Dora brought her a variety of gowns and silky underthings, which the young assistant helped her try on. Tori worried about how long she was taking until they told her Roger had gone to the tavern for a drink. Once she knew he wasn't trapped and bored on the warehouse floor, she eagerly embraced the opportunity to expand her wardrobe. She liked nice clothes, but since money had always been a concern, she'd tended to purchase a few high-quality items and then pair them with inexpensive accessories or one-of-a-kind items she found at thrift stores. She used a similar strategy here, choosing a simple but stunning gown for the evening, a delicate chemise, a serviceable corset, and a few wraps to add warmth. She would blend in better once the weather warmed and she could put away her coat.

Tori realized with some dismay that she was actually contemplating a future in the nineteenth century. Just because the strange woman in the voodoo shop said the power was gone from her necklace didn't mean it was true.

It took a few hours, but when Tori left the dress shop she carried a parcel of underwear and the assurance that her dress would be delivered to her hotel in time for dinner the next day. Roger had returned from the tavern and was waiting for her.

"Do you want to go anywhere else?"

"Can we take the long way back to the hotel?" Tori had only a few coins left and didn't want to spend any more money, but she would like to see more of the town.

Roger obliged, taking her to the cathedral and past some of the homes where the wealthy citizens lived before returning her to the hotel.

Once in her room, Tori called for a bath. As she waited for the servants, she noticed that Jenny had repacked her bags. "I can't believe you're leaving tomorrow." The reality of nineteenth century transportation struck her anew. "I might never see you again."

"You must let me know when you get settled." Jenny wrote something on a slip of paper and handed it to her. "This is my cousin's address in Richmond. Write me there."

Tori tucked the paper into her shabby valise.

"I bathed earlier, so I will give you some privacy. I need to pick up a few items at the shops anyway. This is your last chance to change your mind and come with me."

"Thank you, but my life is here." If, as she feared, she was trapped in the past, St. Louis was more home than Virginia. And she couldn't leave Sebastien no matter how fond she had grown of Jenny.

Jenny gave her a sad smile. "He is a good man," she said, slipping out as the servants entered with ewers of steaming water. Once they were gone, Tori removed her clothes and sank into the blissfully warm water. She washed her body and her hair with the scented bar of soap they had also provided, feeling fully clean for the first time in weeks. She stayed in the water until it grew chilly, then stepped out and wrapped herself in a big towel. She sat in front of the fire while her hair dried, not pulling on her hated clothes until Jenny returned. They had dinner delivered to their room and turned in early.

* * *

Tori accompanied Jenny and Roger to the docks early the next morning. The day was brisk and chilly, the sun little more than a hint of scarlet in the sky. Tori gave Jenny a hug.

"No doubt I will come back once the earth stops shaking. Come visit if I end up back in New Madrid." Jenny's eyes were red, but she kept a determined smile on her face as she grabbed her bags and boarded the ship. Tori had the distinct impression that had she not been there, Jenny and Roger's good bye might have been a bit more impassioned.

"We had better get back," Roger said as soon as Jenny disappeared from view. "I've got business to attend to."

Jenny nodded and they walked silently back to the hotel. They parted at the door, Roger returning to the dock and Tori heading up to her room. She had all day to prepare for her date with Sebastien.

Her dress was delivered as promised and she slipped it on. It was rose-colored, trimmed at the hem and bodice with flowers. Like most gowns of the period, it was high-waisted and looked like something you might see on a Greek statue. She also had wine brought to the room and, on a whim, slipped a pinch of the love potion into it. She didn't believe it would really work, but surely such a small amount wouldn't do any harm. As the time grew close, she draped a shawl around her shoulders.

Sebastien knocked on her door on time and escorted her to the restaurant. It was fairly small compared to what Tori was used to in her time, but the tables, lit by candles and covered with linen cloths, seemed familiar. A waiter, dressed in black, showed them to an empty table and handed them menus. Unlike the plastic menus of her day, these were hand written on heavy paper. To her delight, the choices were listed in French, English, and Spanish.

Sebastien suggested she try the gumbo, so she did. The waiter poured them each a glass of wine and then vanished, leaving them in full view of other diners, but able to speak privately.

"You look lovely."

"Thank you." Sebastien also looked well. He wore the same black coat and brown breeches he had worn to the dance in New Madrid, but had added a ruby red stickpin to the folds of his neck cloth. "And thank you for the dress. I hope to find a way to repay you—"

He cut her off with a wave of his hand. "Unnecessary. Did you enjoy seeing the city?"

Tori suspected, from the hard line of Sebastien's jaw, that Roger had told him about taking her to the voodoo shop. "Very much." She took a sip of her wine for courage. "I went to a magic shop and asked the owner about my necklace. She said the magic was gone. I didn't say what it did, of course, and neither did she, so she might have been

> 173

pretending and not known anything about it at all. But the look in her eyes..." She shivered.

"I wouldn't put much stock in anything she said. Some of these women have the Sight, some just a skill with herbs. But I doubt she has had any experience with a device such as your necklace."

"But I've tried to get it to work and nothing happened."

Their bowls of gumbo arrived with a basket of fresh bread and butter. Sebastien waited until the waiter had served their food and refilled their glasses before speaking. "Would it be so bad, staying here?"

"I want to show you something." Tori fished her cell phone out of her pocket. Like the necklace, she had kept it close, not wanting anyone from this time to see it. It didn't work. Not only was there no service in the nineteenth century, but it had become waterlogged from her dunking in the river. She slipped the flat rectangular object across the table.

Sebastien picked it up. "It's heavier than it looks. What is it?"

"It's a cell phone, which is better than a telephone, which is better than a telegraph, none of which you have in this time."

Sebastien pushed the button on her iPhone, but nothing happened.

"It doesn't work. Getting wet ruined it. Most of the functions wouldn't work anyway because there is no service here and by now it would have lost its charge."

"I don't know what you're talking about."

"I know. Let me explain. Sometime this century, I don't remember when, the telegraph will be invented. This allows operators, using a code, to send messages from one end of the country to another, almost instantly, as long as they are connected by wires."

"Wires?"

"Electrical wires." Tori sighed. This was all so complicated. "I guess electricity must be invented before the telegraph."

"Electricity is lightning."

Tori glanced up. She hadn't expected him to know that, but then she remembered hearing about Ben Franklin and his kite experiments in the eighteenth century. "Yes, but in my time, we have learned to harness the energy, to make it and bring it, through wires, to people's houses."

"How can this be?"

Tori laughed. "I don't know. You don't have to know how it works to use it. In my house I flick a switch and lights turn on. I don't have to rely on candles and they provide much brighter light. I have a furnace which heats the air in my house, like a fire that lights itself. And in the summer, I have an air conditioner which makes the air cool."

"It sounds impossible." Tori couldn't tell from his impassive expression whether or not he believed her.

"I know, but it all comes down to electricity."

"Harnessing the power of lightning. Like Zeus."

"I guess, but it's not magic. Anyway, the telegraph allowed messages to be sent from station to station, but they still had to be hand-delivered to the recipient. When the telephone was invented, it allowed people to speak directly to the other person, without having to turn the message into code, transmit it, turn it back into words, and then get it to the right person. Any two people who had a phone could talk to one another, but it was all connected by wires. The cell phone took away the need for wires. Voices are transmitted through the air, by cell towers, and end up on the other person's phone. Don't ask me how, because I have no idea."

"So you can use this device to talk to another person even if they are far away?" Sebastien sounded skeptical.

"Yes, if hadn't been ruined and if there were cell towers and other cell phones for it to connect to. If it still worked, I could show you some amazing things, but I couldn't call anyone." Or connect to the Internet, but she thought she had given Sebastien enough to think about for one day.

"What else could it do?"

"Take pictures." She held up a hand before he could interrupt. "Now, you have to have an artist paint your portrait, if you want future generations to know what you looked like. Photography will also be invented this century. This allows someone with a camera to take a photograph. Again, I don't know how it all works, but using light and special paper and chemicals, they can preserve your likeness without having to paint it. It's much quicker than painting, but still very slow compared to the kind of pictures my phone used to be able to take. My phone took digital pictures. It didn't need film, and before you ask, I have no more idea how it works than you do."

"These magical devices—they are the reason you want to return?"

"I already told you they're not magical. It's science and technology. I do miss modern conveniences, but our advances have done more than just make life more comfortable. Medicine has greatly improved. Doctors no longer do barbaric things like bleed you when you're sick. Many of the diseases that kill lots of people in your time, like smallpox, are completely gone in mine."

"So people live a long time."

"Life expectancy is greater than now, but there are still bad diseases and people still get old. We haven't found the Fountain of Youth—yet."

Sebastien stared at her as he reached for another slice of bread. "I, too, would like to experience such wonders. And what of the family you left behind? They must be worried about you."

"No family. My mother died a few years ago and my father ran off when I was young."

"No husband?"

Tori shook her head. "I might seem like an old maid to you, but it's not unusual to delay marriage in the future."

"Not all girls marry young even now." Sebastien dipped his bread into his soup.

Tori, who had been doing most of the talking, took advantage of his mulling to catch up on her eating. The gumbo was delicious, thick and filling. But after she had satisfied some of her hunger, she grew impatient with his lack of response. "So you see why I must find a way home?"

"No. There is no one waiting for you there, only your scientific miracles."

Tori gaped at him, then remembered her manners and closed her mouth. She supposed it was too much to expect Sebastien to understand. The wonders she had described to him were no more than words. He would never understand what it was like to walk into your climate-controlled house, flip a switch and make morning out of night, sit down at your computer and have a world of knowledge at your fingers. And she hadn't even told him about cars or airplanes. "I have friends," she said stiffly. He did have something of a point. Since college, she had allowed many of her friendships to lapse.

"Of course you have friends, Victoria. How could you not? But you have no husband or family."

"I have my career as a music teacher. Well, I did until I got fired."

"I don't know what that means."

"Sorry." Tori searched for another term. "I got sacked. Let go. I'm unemployed."

"Why would he sack you? I've heard how well you play."

"I had a disagreement with one of my student's parents—the man I think may have forced me into the river, but I'm not sure."

Sebastien's mouth tightened. "Why would you want to return to a time that doesn't seem to appreciate you?"

"I don't have the skills to survive here. All I can do is play the violin."

Sebastien reached across the table and took her hand. "You underestimate yourself. Many people of this time cannot even read and write. You have an education. You could always teach."

"I guess, but women have no rights in this time. That scares me more than the primitive state of medicine and the lack of electricity and plumbing."

"Enough of this. I have saddened you and that was not my intention. New Orleans is a beautiful city. Where would you like to go after dinner?"

Tori leaned forward and told him.

Chapter 21

They slipped inside Tori's hotel room and Sebastien closed the door behind him. "Are you sure?"

No, Tori thought, as she gave him a wobbly grin. By inviting Sebastien back to her room, she was breaking the rules of a proper unmarried lady in this time, but if she was to learn to live here, she must find her own way. "I've wanted this almost from the moment you plucked me from the river."

"As have I. You are a beautiful woman, Victoria."

Some men would have taken advantage of her perilous situation, alone in a strange land without resources. Not Sebastien. He might be a river rogue, but he was not without honor. She suppressed a shiver at the thought of Ned's hands on her groping and pawing. Sebastien was not Ned. She had lived on his boat for weeks. He could have overpowered her at any time and his men, with the possible exception of Roger, would have looked the other way. She felt the heat of his body as he came up behind her and drew her into his embrace. She stiffened momentarily. Not only had she let friendships lapse, she'd rarely had time for romantic entanglements. It had been a long time since she'd been with a man and even longer since she'd desired someone as she did Sebastien. It wasn't just his looks, although his powerful body and chiseled features drew her eyes. He had saved her life and looked after her since.

He spun her within the circle of his arms so they were face to face. He, too, had taken pains with his appearance and the scruffy beard she was used to had vanished, replaced by a square jaw. She ran her fingers along his jaw and then trailed them across his lips.

"You clean up well."

His laughter was a low rumble in his chest. "My mother always insisted upon my father and I being clean-shaven at home. While in the woods or on the river we could do as we pleased, but once we were home, we had to become civilized again."

A wise woman.

Sebastien bent his head to hers and tasted her lips. His were warm and firm, but not as rough as she would have expected from days spent in the harsh elements. He nibbled at her and then grew bolder, capturing her mouth with his.

Yes. Tori flattened herself against his hard chest. He was rock solid, and even through his shirt she could feel the ridges of muscle. She played with his neck cloth, tugging at it until it came undone. She pulled it loose, marveling at its length. A steady pulse beat in his throat to match her own. Her hands grew restless once more and reached for his coat, pushing it off his shoulders. He was wearing far too many clothes.

Sebastien obliged her by shrugging free of the restrictive garment and allowing her to toss it to the floor. Her own wrap had been discarded as soon as she entered the room. Her head fell back as he moved on to her neck, and she whimpered softly. She made no protest as his fingers fumbled with the back fastenings of her gown, puzzling out their mystery and at last freeing her from the elegant, expensive gown.

Shyness reared its head when she stood before him in only her corset and shift while he was still fully dressed. Well, without his coat, which would be scandalous in these times, but was more covered up than most men of her own time generally dressed. He still wore a shirt, a waistcoat, a neck cloth and breeches. Instinctively she tried to cover herself and he took pity on her.

"Shall we have some wine?" he asked, stepping away from her..

"That sounds lovely," she said and tried to gather her scattered nerves while he poured from the bottle the hotel had left in her room.

She'd had a sip before dinner and enjoyed it. While she still felt at times that she would sell her soul for a Diet Pepsi, she had grown used to drinking alcohol with almost every meal.

She sat on the bed and slipped her shoes off. When he handed her a glass, she gulped down half the contents.

"Whoa. There's no need to be nervous."

Easy for you to say. "I'm not," she said, but her voice came out in a squeak. Sebastien took the glass from her and set it on the nightstand next to his own. He removed his boots in a practiced motion, then knelt on the bed, easing her back against the pillows. She worked on the buttons of his shirt as he kissed her, but they only went part way down. "How do you undo this?"

Sebastien pulled away, slipped off his waistcoat and pulled his shirt over his head.

"Oh." Tori blushed at her lack of knowledge and the sight of his chest, which screamed 'six pack.' "The buttons should go all the way down." Her embarrassment vanished at the sight of the feast in front of her. She tried to pull him close, but he was having none of it. He made short work of her corset and followed with her shift. Only then did he allow her to pull him down on the bed.

She touched him, hands exploring, and he did the same. She ran her fingers from his flat stomach and up toward his collar bone. She hesitated as she noticed the jagged scar near his right breast. After a moment, she ran her fingers over it, feeling the puckered skin.

"Arrow."

Her hand jerked back. "Indians?"

"From the first trip my father and I took out west. Beaver was growing scarce along the Missouri so we went farther afield. All the way out to the Rockies. I'd love to show you those mountains, some day. They are beautiful, but it's rough country. Some of the tribes had never seen a white man, although most had been trading with the French-Canadians for years. My father had traded there as a young man, but we were trapping, cutting out the middleman, and some of the Indians didn't like that."

Tori had been to the Rockies. She'd gone skiing with a group of friends from college. But she hadn't seen them in this time, before man had civilized them. "I would like to see them, but I don't want to be shot with an arrow. How did you survive?"

"My father got it out, cleaned the wound and bandaged it up. The rest is up to luck and God's grace."

And somehow avoiding infection. She pressed her lips to the scar, struck by how she could have lost him before ever meeting him. Life was short in any time, but the lack of antibiotics, anesthesia and sterile medical practices made it doubly so in this one.

"You can't head west without risk," he said, seeming to sense her disquiet. "But I know what I'm doing."

She didn't doubt that. Shaking her head, she tried to dismiss the worries from her mind. There was plenty of time for that later. "Show me," she said in a teasing voice.

He gave a mock growl and fastened his mouth on her neck, marking her. She gasped as sensations slid down her spine. His hands, though rough with callouses, were gentle as they skimmed down her body. Everywhere he touched, her nerve endings awoke to ravenous pleasure. When he reached her most sensitive area and stroked her soft folds, she dug her head into the pillow, searching, seeking.

He murmured something in French and his hand disappeared. Seconds later, he returned, having dispensed with his breeches. For the first time she could feel all of him, in all his glorious masculinity. His legs were as heavily muscled as the rest of him, and lightly furred with dark hair. His erection pulsed hot and heavy against her stomach, tantalizing her and filling her with a curious feminine satisfaction. He wanted her as much as she wanted him.

"I've dreamed of you," he murmured before he took her breast in his mouth, sucking gently. He raised his head and continued. "The thought of you in my bed haunted me."

"I've dreamed of you, as well." Lying in his berth, surrounded by his masculine scent.

He rolled over her, spreading her legs with his. It felt right. Her past boyfriends seemed little more than boys as she gazed into his fierce eyes. Sebastien was a man in every sense of the word.

He whispered something—a French endearment, she guessed—then slid inside her. She felt her body stretch to accommodate him and then he moved, slowly at first, but with ever-greater speed. She met his thrusts with joyful abandon. His breath grew labored and he murmured once more something she couldn't understand. She grew taut, reaching, and then suddenly she shattered, sensation exploding throughout her body. Sebastien followed her seconds later, pumping within her before collapsing atop her. He stayed there only for a moment, before switching their positions and relieving her of his weight. He gathered her close before pulling the covers over their bodies and blowing out the candle.

"Sleep, Victoria mine."

She smiled, her body singing, but deliciously relaxed. She would sleep, better than she had in weeks. But she thought with a pang that she couldn't truly be his. Not when they came from such different worlds.

CHAPTER 22

Sebastien settled his business in New Orleans faster than he would have thought possible, making a tidy profit. So many boats had been lost during the earthquakes that goods were in high demand. It was a blip in the market, not a sign of long-term opportunity, but if Victoria was right in her predictions that still more earthquakes were to come, the market might remain profitable for some time. He was unlikely to benefit from it, however—it would take months to slowly propel the *Fury* upstream. By then, surely the earthquakes would be over.

He almost wished it had taken longer to dispose of his cargo, for he spent every night in Victoria's bed, exploring every inch of her body until he knew it better than he knew his own. Her response delighted him, but one thing troubled him. He had kept it to himself until now, but eventually he would have to confront her. He had not been her first lover.

He and Roger spent their last day in New Orleans rounding up the men. Most were found in brothels, some in dingy taverns and one in the absinthe house. All were ordered to get cleaned up and ready to report for duty the next morning.

He had already arranged with Victoria and the hotel to eat a private dinner in her room. She planned to spend their last day in civilization picking up creams, lotions and other feminine necessities. She was familiar enough with the city that she insisted upon going by herself, which worried Sebastien—not so much because he thought she would encounter danger, but because he suspected she wanted to visit yet another voodoo shop to ask about the necklace. It seemed to him that the necklace was dead, if it had in fact ever had anything to do with her spectacular journey, but even the chance that it might be capable of taking her away from him made him uneasy.

He hadn't seen her since he left her that morning, still sleeping, so he was anxious for their meeting and looking forward to giving her a gift he'd had specially commissioned for her, and dreading the conversation he knew they had to have. She responded almost immediately to his knock, swinging the door open and giving him her shy smile.

"The food should be here soon." She had drawn two chairs up to the small round table in her room. A bottle of wine already waited there. She glanced curiously at his package, but when he set it aside and began pouring the wine, she didn't ask him what was in it.

"To us," he said, handing her a glass.

"To us," she repeated and they clinked their glasses.

"Did you get everything you needed today?"

"I suppose so. Of course once we get on the river, I will remember what I've forgotten. No matter, I had next to nothing coming down."

He couldn't tell from her response whether or not she had gone in search of more answers. "I always hate to leave New Orleans." Never more so than this time.

She tilted her head to one side. "Don't you want to get home?"

"The journey upriver is difficult. It will be months before we see St. Louis."

A knock on the door signaled the arrival of their food. The waiter took his time setting up the bread, and the plates of roast beef, mashed potatoes and gravy. Sebastien hadn't eaten since breakfast and it smelled wonderful. They took their seats and began eating, talking of inconsequential things until most of the food had disappeared. Only then did Sebastien reach for the package he had brought.

"I got something for you."

Victoria's cheeks reddened. "You've already done so much for me. You didn't need to buy me a gift."

"Wait until you see it. You might change your mind."

"It's heavy," she said as she took the package from him. She removed the wrappings, gasping when she saw what was inside.

"Go on, try it out."

The paper fell to the floor as Victoria pulled the object from it. She set the wooden case on the table and opened it carefully. "It's lovely, every bit as beautiful as my old violin that perished in the river." Her fingers caressed the smooth wood, fiddled with the knobs, and plucked at the strings.

"Play something for me."

She nestled the violin under her chin and drew the bow across the strings. After a few minutes of warming up, she played the same song she had played the night she had charmed his men. When she finished, she looked up at him, her eyes dancing. "Now for something more modern." She began to play again, and a tune such as he had never heard before filled the small room.

"Something from your time?"

"From a band known as the Beatles. Very popular group, but they broke up long before I was born. People still play their music, though." She set the violin aside. "Thank you, Sebastien. I don't know if I will ever be able to repay you. I'm sure this was very expensive."

"It's a gift." Maybe even a bribe, if he admitted it.

Her blue eyes lit with warmth. "I will treasure it always."

"There is something I've been meaning to ask you."

"I'll tell you what I can, but remember, I was a music major, not a history major. Besides, I still worry about contaminating the time line."

Sebastien laughed. "No, this is personal, between you and me."

Her brow wrinkled, then smoothed out. "Ask away."

"I know you want to return to your own time, but that might not be possible. I want you to stay with me. I can guide you through things you find confusing and keep you safe and protected."

"I would like to stay with you as well, but I'm not sure I'm cut out for life on the river. And what about when you go trapping? Will you take me with you?"

"I would set you up in a house in St. Louis and hire a few servants to take care of things. You could still travel with me on the river if I upgrade the living quarters. It's not unusual for flatboat operators to bring their whole family with them." She had grown still as he talked and the warm light had faded from her eyes, leaving them cool.

"You want me to be your mistress."

Sebastien had not wanted to phrase his offer in exactly those terms. "I mean you no insult. I just don't want you to worry about the future."

She laughed, but the sound was brittle. "How can I not be insulted by your offer to make me a kept woman?"

He had not expected this level of resistance. "We are already together, Victoria. I thought only to formalize the arrangement to give you security."

"I didn't invite you back to my room because I wanted to be your mistress, I invited you because I had feelings for you."

"Feelings that I share." Sebastien stood and began to pace the room. What did she want from him? He had never set up a mistress before, preferring fleeting moments with professionals. He had thought the house and servants a generous offer, but perhaps she wanted more. "I will bring you other gifts. Jewels and such."

Her posture grew more rigid. "I think you had better go."

"Fine." This was not going at all how he had anticipated. "Be ready to leave tomorrow."

"I'm not sure I'll be going with you."

"What else will you do? Stay here? How will you survive?"

"You were willing to abandon me in Ste. Genevieve. Why not here? As to how I will survive—that's none of your business."

"Father Andre had found a family for you to stay with. I was not abandoning you to starve."

"How generous. They were willing to give me room and board to be their unpaid nursemaid."

"New Orleans is a beautiful and prosperous city, but it also has a corrupt underbelly. I am not leaving you here, Victoria."

She began gathering the dishes from their dinner and piling them into the hallway. "You can't force me to come with you."

"Think about it and be ready to leave when I come for you," Sebastien said before storming out of the room, out of the hotel, and into the cool crisp January evening.

Chapter 23

Sebastien awoke to a pounding head and a deep sense of loss. He knew at once he had drunk too much the night before, and at first he suspected he had lost a pile at the gaming tables, although he rarely gambled. As he sat up, however, his stomach lurched and he remembered the scene with Victoria. He had lost something more valuable than money, and still had no notion what he had done wrong. He thought she would be happy to have her future secured since it appeared unlikely she would return to her own time. He hadn't even brought up the subject of her previous lovers, as he had intended.

He sent a maid downstairs for a pot of strong coffee, but couldn't face food. He drank two cups as he dressed and splashed cold water on his face, then went to meet Roger at the docks.

A few of the men had already reported for duty, looking little better than Sebastien felt, and Roger had them busily loading the small cargo they would be taking upstream. They would carry a few luxury goods to St. Louis and the other towns along the river, but it was hard enough to move the boat itself against the current. It would be impossible with a heavy load.

"Good morning," Roger said, sounding irritatingly cheerful. "The cargo and supplies are nearly on board and the way the men are trickling in, we should be able to cast off by midmorning."

"Good. I'll take over here. I want you to gather up the stragglers and help Victoria get her things on board."

Roger gave him a searching look, seeming to linger on his bloodshot eyes. "Why wouldn't you help her on board?"

"She's angry with me. Might not even sail with us."

"What else would she do? She knows no one here."

"Exactly what I told her, but you know women. Just go get her. You can talk her around."

"Let's grab a cup of coffee."

"I already had some at the hotel."

"Yeah, so did I, but I need another."

Sebastien sensed a lecture coming. "Very well," he muttered, heading toward the small galley. A pot of the nasty black sludge that served for coffee on the river sat on the stove. He splashed a bit into two cups and slumped into a chair. "Get on with it."

Roger drank a bit of the coffee and wiped his mouth with his hand. "Puts that fancified stuff you get at the hotel to shame."

Sebastien glared at him, his coffee untouched. He worried his stomach would rebel if he tried to drink it.

"What did you do to that sweet girl?"

"Nothing. I didn't hurt her. We never found the group she was traveling with. Might have perished on the river during the earthquakes, for all we know. I didn't want her to worry about what might happen to her, so I thought I would formalize our relationship." He didn't like lying to Roger, but wouldn't betray Victoria's trust and share her secret. Roger probably wouldn't believe him anyway. Sebastien still wasn't sure he believed it himself.

"You asked her to marry you?"

Sebastien scowled. Roger sounded more like a gossipy girl than a hard scrabble riverman. "'Course not. Do I look like the marrying type to you? I'm wed to the river and the wilderness."

"Then what, exactly, did you ask of her?"

Why was he feeling so guilty? She had known from the first the type of life he led. "I told her I would get her a house in St. Louis and take care of her."

"I haven't spent as much time with her as you have, but even I know she ain't no whore."

Sebastien stood so quickly the chair toppled over behind him. "Of course she's not a whore. So help me, Roger, if you weren't my friend and nearly old enough to be my father I'd pop you one for that."

"Then why'd you go and treat her like one?"

"I didn't," he protested, but even to his own ears it sounded weak. Had she expected him to offer marriage? He picked up the chair and leaned against it. "Just go get her. Once we're on the river, I can patch things up."

Roger snorted. "I'll try to fix your mess, but Miss Foster has a mind of her own. It may already be too late."

* * *

The voodoo shop looked much the same as it had the first time she'd visited it. The potent smell of spices mingled with a vague stench of death. A dead chicken, missing its head, sprawled across a shrine in a corner, and skulls and bones hung from the ceiling. In contrast, jars and bottles lined the shelves in neat rows. Tori gagged at the sight of the chicken and hoped she wouldn't be sick.

"You're back," the woman said.

"Yes. Are you sure you cannot help me? You implied that you could... for a price."

"I told you that all magic comes with a price. That is all. It would take very dark magic to animate the necklace."

Tori wondered if she was prepared for 'very dark magic' when even the sight of a dead chicken made her sick. Still, when she remembered the way Sebastien had treated her, she felt desperate to escape the confines of the nineteenth century. "I am ready."

The woman looked offended. "I do not practice dark magic."

"What's that?" Tori cocked her head toward the bloody display.

"A sacrifice to the gods, a time-honored tradition."

Tori guessed that was true. And it wasn't like she was a vegetarian or anything, but she preferred her chickens without feathers. "Do you know of someone who does practice dark magic?"

"I would not tell you if I did. I don't want you to get in trouble."

Tori bit down on her bottom lip. "I can take care of myself."

The woman smirked. "How did the love potion work?"

"Fine," Tori said, although the thought of it now made her nauseous. Sebastien didn't love her and never had.

"I think not, or you wouldn't be back."

"The man I was interested in turned out not to be worth it."

"That is not the fault of the potion."

"Don't worry. I'm not here for a refund."

"All sales are final."

"I figured," Tori muttered under her breath as she walked out. Where to next? There were other voodoo shops, but she felt as if she could still smell the congealed blood and figured the woman was right. Dark magic was out of her league and would only lead to trouble. So, if she was stuck in this century and could no longer depend on Sebastien, she had to get a job. And there was only one thing she had ever been good at.

* * *

Tori sat at the third tavern she'd been to, nursing a brandy in the corner. *Three strikes and you're out.* She took a deep swallow. She had played nightclubs before, heard a lot of lousy pickup lines, and evaded wandering hands, but never had the club owners taken it for granted that she would sleep with them in order to be allowed to play in their bar. She had a few more places to try, but wasn't hopeful. If this didn't work, she would have to try teaching, but had no idea how to go about finding a teaching position.

She saw a pair of boots approach, but didn't feel up to fending off any more unwanted advances. "Bug off," she said without looking up.

"That any way to treat an old friend?"

Tori raised her head at the familiar voice. "Roger? I'd have thought you would be gone by now."

"Still rounding up the stragglers. You included."

"I'm not coming."

"That's what Sebastien said, but I'm not buying it. This is no place for a nice girl like you."

"I don't have a place."

"Your place is on the *Fury*."

"Not anymore."

"Whatever happened between you and Sebastien is between the two of you. If you don't want to be with him any more, that's fine. But I own part of that boat and I want you to come along as the fiddler."

Being back on the Fury sounded better than being out on the street. She had no car or Walmart parking lot to sleep in. "Sebastien know about this?"

"He don't need to know everything I do."

"I can hardly hide on a keelboat, especially if I'm going to be playing the violin."

"You won't have to hide. You can have my room."

After the way she had been treated today, Tori no longer had the energy to be angry with Sebastien. For the standards of the time, her behavior had led him to believe she was a fallen woman and he had acted accordingly. His feelings for her weren't as strong as hers were for him, but in his own way he had given her a fair shake. "Okay, Roger, you have a deal."

"What does the word 'okay' mean?"

Oops, guess it hasn't been invented yet. "It's just a silly expression that's starting to catch on back East."

"I like it. So, did you leave your things at the hotel?"

"No." Tori hefted her bag. "It's all in here." Even her new violin was nestled inside, along with her clothes. She remembered all the boxes she'd carried into Ned's apartment and stuffed into her car. She felt sad that everything she now owned could fit in a single bag, but in some ways it was freeing.

Roger offered her his arm and they headed back to the boat.

Chapter 24

Sebastien reluctantly moved his things back into his cabin when it became obvious that Victoria would no longer stay there. She moved into Roger's cabin and did her best to avoid Sebastien for the first few days of the journey upriver. On such a small craft, however, it was impossible not to have any contact. So although she took her meals with Roger and spent the days hanging out by the stove, he still saw her every day and sometimes caught a whiff of the perfume she had bought in New Orleans when they were in close quarters. The best times, though, were when she brought out the violin he had given her and played rousing songs for the men.

Except on the rare days when there was sufficient wind to raise the sail, travel upstream was slow and laborious. Where the river was shallow enough, the men used poles to propel the boat forward. The teams were changed out regularly, for the work was brutal and frequent rest was required. Since Roger was too old for poling, he took Sebastien's place on the roof when Sebastien was at the poles, and another of their most experienced and trusted men took the helm. Sebastien prided himself on taking regular shifts, unlike some of the patrons. The work kept his body fit and toned, and by working alongside the men he earned their respect.

Victoria began sitting with Roger while he was on roof duty and after about a week afloat, she remained once Sebastien took over.

"I'm glad you decided to take the position of fiddler," he said. "I've never had one before, but the men enjoy it."

"I didn't have much of a choice. Employment prospects in New Orleans looked bleak."

Sebastien had told her as much, but didn't think she would appreciate him saying that. He cast a sideways glance at her. She looked to be in good health, the gritty determination which had seen her downriver still evident, but the spark that had infused her while in New Orleans had vanished. His fault, he realized.

"Don't get me wrong. I'm glad to be back on the *Fury*. Seems more like home than anywhere else in this time."

"Once we get to St. Louis, you can decide whether or not you want to stay on as our fiddler or find work there. My stepmother would be able to get you settled somewhere." She'd find something for Victoria or risk losing the stipend he paid her.

"Thank you." She sighed, reached over and took his gloved hand in hers. "I'm no longer angry at you. You're a man of your time and I'm a woman of mine. I can't accept the arrangement you offered because I'm used to being treated more or less as an equal. Things still are far from perfect in the twenty-first century, but women have rights there. They can even vote."

"Vote?" Sebastien asked in astonishment. Surely she was exaggerating. He couldn't imagine men ever giving women the power to influence government.

"Yes, though it took a ridiculously long time. It's more than a century away, but eventually it happens."

No wonder she wanted to return to her own world. Sebastien himself was tempted by the wonders she had described. "Tell me more," he urged.

"Being a man, you would probably be interested in cars."

"Cars?"

"Horseless carriages. Vehicles that run on gasoline, a liquid fuel. Most adults own one and can travel anywhere. Paved roads makes it quick and easy."

"What about river traffic?"

"It still exists, but steamboats, like The New Orleans, will replace keelboats and flatboats before too long.

Then there are airplanes."

Sebastien raised his brows.

"Crafts that fly through the air, carrying people and cargo. You can travel from the East Coast to the West in a matter of hours instead of months."

Sebastien wondered if she was pulling his leg. Flying vehicles? It seemed impossible. "Is this really true? How could ships fly through the air?"

She shrugged. "Once again, I can't explain the technology."

"But time travel is still a mystery?"

"Oh, yes. I didn't believe in time travel until I experienced it myself." She fell silent after that and Sebastien assumed she was thinking about the future, which was her past. It was all very confusing.

They fell back into their old routine as the days passed, but Victoria remained somewhat aloof. Hoping to break through her reserve and liven up their diet, which was growing tedious again as the fresh food they had picked up in New Orleans was consumed, Sebastien decided to head up a hunting trip. He picked a few men to accompany him and asked Victoria to come along as well.

"I don't know anything about guns or hunting."

"I'm not expecting you to catch anything, I just thought you might like to get off the boat for a few hours."

"That does sound tempting." She pondered for a few minutes, then gave him a smile. "I'm in."

They brought the boat ashore, lowered the gangplank and dispersed the hunters. Roger would be in charge until Sebastien returned.

The group split in two, one heading north and the other west. Dalton, the *Fury*'s former, unofficial fiddler, ended up paired with Sebastien and Victoria, a situation Sebastien would have preferred to avoid since the man still seemed to hold some resentment toward Victoria. As soon as they set off, Sebastien drew Victoria back under the guise of teaching her how to walk quietly. She proved a poor pupil, seeming to step on every branch in their path.

"Guess I'll never make a good hunter."

Dalton was a distance away, but Sebastien lowered his voice just to be sure. "I suppose there's no need to be where you come from."

"No need, but people do it for fun. They eat their kills; it's not wasted, but you can buy anything you need at the store."

A shot rang out from ahead of them and Victoria flinched. Sebastien looked over and saw Dalton had bagged a rabbit. He picked up the dead animal and placed it in his pouch. They continued on, falling silent so as not to scare the game any more than Victoria's heavy footsteps did. They had not gone very far, when they stumbled upon a homestead.

"Should we go around?" Dalton asked.

"I brought a few coins with me and they might have something they'd be willing to sell or trade for that rabbit. Worth a shot," Sebastien said. They started across the field, which had been cleared of trees but showed signs of crops having been grown there during the summer. Now it was little more than stubble, but they followed a plume of smoke they could see in the distance.

A cabin stood beyond the rise, small but sturdy. The chimney lay in ruins, a victim of the quakes. Sebastien shouted a greeting as they approached the cabin. The door opened and a man stepped out, pointing a rifle directly at them.

"Go away. We don't cotton to strangers here."

Sebastien stowed his gun and held up his hands. "We can go, but we mean you no harm. Thought you might like to talk a spot of business."

The mention of business made the man lower his rifle just a tad. "What kind of business?"

"I'm a riverboat man and I've got money if you have fresh food to sell."

"Got whiskey."

"I'm afraid we don't need any whiskey. Looking for a chicken, eggs, cheese, something like that."

"Most of my chickens ran off after my wife died, but I've still got some cheese." He pushed the cabin door open with his foot. "Bessie, go to the spring house and get a wheel of cheese." A young black woman exited the cabin and gave the three strangers a frightened look. She said nothing, heading into the woods, presumably to get the cheese.

"I've got a bad feeling about this," Victoria whispered in his ear.

Sebastien nodded slightly, for he agreed. They should have steered clear of the homestead.

"I'll take some of that whiskey if you have it handy," Dalton said.

The farmer narrowed his eyes at them, then stepped inside the cabin, returning with a jug and some cups. He filled one of the cups, then turned to Sebastien. "You and the girl want some?"

"No, thank you," Sebastien said. The cups looked like they hadn't been washed since they'd been brought west. Dalton didn't seem to care. He drained his cup and smacked his lips appreciatively.

"Powerful stuff. You got a nice place here."

"It's a dump. All gone to hell since the old lady died. Then the earthquakes come and knock down my chimney. You ask me, it's a sign, a sign that we don't belong here and should all go back East."

"Sounds like you've fallen on hard times. Better keep your cheese. Might need it later." Sebastien turned to go.

The gun came up. "Stop right there. You said you had money."

"A few coins."

"I want to see them."

Moving carefully, to avoid suspicion, Sebastien reached into his pocket and pulled out a handful of coins. He opened his hand so the old man could see.

The man grunted. "Reckon that'll do."

Alerted by something in the man's manner, Sebastien dropped the money and went for his gun, but he wasn't fast enough. The farmer fired, and red-hot flame tore through Sebastien's shoulder. He fell to the ground as the sound of another gunshot echoed through the air. Dalton. He hoped he had made his shot.

Victoria screamed and fell to her knees by his side. "Sebastien!"

"I'm all right. Help me up." She helped him to a sitting position, letting him lean against her for support. Sebastien gritted his teeth at the searing pain. "The farmer?"

"Dalton got him."

"He should have known that would happen... two to one."

"I think he passed crazy two exits back."

It hurt too much to ponder out Victoria's strange way of talking. "Dalton... help me back to the boat."

"Not gonna happen."

Sebastien looked up through bleary eyes. His crewman stood over him, gun reloaded and pointed at his head. "What are you doing?"

"Step away from Sebastien, Victoria."

"No!"

"Do it." Dalton's voice was ice cold and the gun never wavered. "I don't want to shoot him. He wasn't all that bad a boss, but I will if I have to."

Fear swept across Sebastien, lending him a smidgen of strength. Dalton wanted Victoria. Sebastien couldn't let that happen. He lurched to his feet. "Run, Victoria!" And he launched himself at Dalton.

Chapter 25

"Run, Victoria!" Sebastien shouted as he threw himself at their turncoat crewman. She wanted to. Her heart pounded, geared up for flight, but she seemed frozen in place.

The gun went off again and this time when Sebastien fell, he stayed down, blood darkening the red of his shirt. "You killed him and for what? Because I took your job as fiddler?"

"Stupid bitch."

The blow seemed to come out of nowhere, cracking across her jaw and flinging her to the ground. She scrambled in the dirt trying to regain her feet, but a kick sent her sprawling once more. He came after her, kneeling on her chest and ripping at her dress. Had she escaped rape in the twenty-first century only to experience it in the nineteenth?

He bared her throat and yanked, breaking the chain around her neck. Shoving the necklace in his pocket, he took off into the woods.

Tori gulped air into her lungs. Her face throbbed from where he had hit her and her ribs ached from his kick. Shaking, she picked herself up and stumbled over to Sebastien, falling on her knees beside him. He lay still and unmoving, his face pale. Dalton had wanted the damn necklace. It must have been he who spied on them at Christmas. He'd killed Sebastien for a chance to time travel.

"I'm sorry," she said, tears running down her face and splashing on his bloody shirt. "I didn't mean to bring danger into your life."

"You didn't."

Tori's eyes flew to his face. He was still alive! "Sebastien, I need to get help. I'll get Roger. He'll know what to do." The sheer enormity of her situation hit her. Sebastien had been shot twice. He was severely, possibly critically injured and she was miles from the boat, unsure if she could even find her way back.

"Yes, get Roger." His eyes fluttered. "Help me to the cabin, then go."

She couldn't carry him. He weighed a great deal more than she did. But he was right. She couldn't leave him here lying in a pool of his own blood. "I can drag you," she said, though the thought of the damage that might do to him made her wince.

"Support me. I'll walk," Sebastien said through gritted teeth.

Tori hauled him once more to a sitting position and crouching beside him, placed her shoulder under his arm. "I'm going to stand." She did so, lifting with her legs as much as possible, as she had been taught. Sebastien cried out, but he came with her, standing on his own two feet, although much of his weight rested on Tori. "Okay, now we'll walk slowly toward the house."

He made a sound she took as assent and she moved forward, trying to carry as much of his weight as she could. His breath came labored, as if he were running a marathon, and she didn't know if they could make it. But she kept at it, pausing every time he seemed to lose consciousness, all the while speaking to him in soothing tones. "You can do it. Almost there." She repeated the litany as much for her as him as they inched toward the cabin.

When they finally reached it, she kicked the door open and shambled inside, Sebastien nearly a dead weight on her back. A bed stood against the wall and she lowered him into it as gently as she could, raising his feet once she had his head and torso situated. "We did it, we made it," she said, her own breath coming hard. Sebastien didn't respond. He had grown even paler than before, his skin white against the black of his scruffy beard, and seemed to have lost consciousness completely. There was no way she could leave him in this condition.

Why hadn't she paid more attention to her mom when she'd talked about her job as a nurse? She found a knife on the counter and cut his shirt open, exposing the wounds in all their bloody gore. She swallowed and closed her eyes until her head stopped spinning. He had been shot twice, once in the shoulder and once in the side. She didn't think the shoulder wound was necessarily fatal, unless the bullet had hit an artery, but the side wound was more problematic. If his intestines were damaged, there was no way he could survive without modern medicine. Even if both bullets had missed vital organs, the chance of infection and death were very high.

A sound from the doorway made her turn. The black woman who had been sent for the cheese stood in the doorway, her eyes wide. Tori still held the knife in her hand. She gripped it more firmly and hoped she wouldn't have to use it.

"The master's dead," the woman said.

"Yes. I'm sorry, but he attacked us. He shot my friend." The woman—Bessie, Tori remembered—glanced over at Sebastien.

"He's always been meaner than spit, but since the earthquakes come and the missus died, well, he's gone plum crazy."

The tension eased slightly in Tori's shoulders. Bessie didn't seem to be mourning the man's death. "My friend is very badly hurt. Can you help?"

Bessie took a closer look. "More'n likely to die."

No! Tori closed her eyes. "I know it looks bad, but I need to do everything I can to save him."

Bessie turned Sebastien slightly, examining his back. "Bullets are still in there. They have to come out."

"Can you do that? Do you know how to get the bullets out?"

Bessie looked at her as if she were crazy. "Never done it before, and I'm sure as hell not gonna be touching no white man now."

"Sebastien's men will come for him, but I don't know how long that will take. Do you think I should wait? I've never removed any bullets either."

"More white folks coming? I need to get out of here."

"Where are you going?"

"North. Canada."

It was a very long way, especially with the constant threat of Indians or slave catchers. "Be careful."

Bessie gave her a strange look. "Take this." She walked over to a rudely constructed hutch on the far wall and grabbed a jar off it. "Dig the bullets out, put this salve on the wounds and bandage him up. Keep him warm and give him something to drink."

Tori took the jar, unscrewed the lid and gazed at the contents in suspicion. The jar was filled with a brown paste and had a pungent smell. The thought of putting it on Sebastien's wounds make her queasy, but maybe it would help.

Bessie grabbed a bed roll off the floor and began filling it with other jars from the hutch as well as the cheese she had brought with her. She rolled it up and slung the improvised pack over her shoulder. She gave Tori a curt nod and ducked out the door.

Tori was alone again and faced with a task she dreaded. Sebastien was still unconscious, however, so the sooner she got the bullets out, the better. She was his only hope of survival. A fire burned in the hearth. She held the knife in the flames to sterilize it. Then she swung the kettle, already filled with water, over the fire, to heat the water. At least she knew how to guard against infection.

While she waited for the water to heat, she tore strips from her petticoat. She wanted to use as little as possible from the cabin since it looked like it hadn't been cleaned since the old man's wife died, or maybe even before that.

Once the water was hot, she poured some into a bowl and grabbed her makeshift bandages and the knife. First she cleaned the blood from the wounds so she could see better. A small hole in his shoulder marked where the bullet had entered. As Bessie had claimed, there was no exit wound. Tori inserted the tip of the knife in the hole and dug in. It was harder than she thought, especially when Sebastien screamed and thrashed on the bed. The knife fell from her fingers onto the floor. Sebastien lay there, moaning, still not fully conscious but obviously aware of the pain she had caused him. Tori felt sick.

She picked the knife off the floor and held it in the flames once more until it glowed red. She carried the knife back over to the bed, gazing down at Sebastien's pale features. Would she need to tie him down? "Sebastien, I need to get the bullets out. Can you hold still for me?"

His eyes opened to slits. "Dalton," he muttered. "Run."

"Dalton's gone. It's just you and me."

"Get back to the boat. Leave me."

"I can't."

"Gonna die anyway."

Tori clamped her lips together. "No, Sebastien. Remember the scar on your chest? Your father got the arrow out and saved you. I'm going to do the same." She felt far less confident than her words, but tried not to let that show.

His eyes met hers, fierce like the eagle he was compared to. "Do it."

She stuck the knife in again and he went rigid, trying to not to flinch away from her fingers. She tried to work fast so as to not prolong his agony, but the wound grew slippery with blood and she didn't know what she was doing. After what seemed like an eternity, she felt something hard against the tip of her knife. She twisted the blade and Sebastien cried out. To her relief, he went limp, and she carefully worked the lead free. She nearly gagged when she dropped the misshapen ball on the floor and she wasn't even finished.

Worried about the amount of blood he was losing, she hesitated, then reached for the jar Bessie had given her. She smeared a generous amount of the paste into the wound and then placed a wad of her bundled up petticoat against it and bound it tightly to his shoulder with additional fabric. Then she turned her attention to the other bullet hole. This wound was shallow, more like a deep gouge along his side and she felt fairly certain it hadn't hit any vital organs. She wasn't even sure the bullet was inside him. After a quick probing, she decided, to her relief, that it was not. She cleaned the wound again, smeared on some of the home remedy and applied a bandage to it as well.

Now all she could do was wait and pray that infection didn't set it and that Sebastien's men came for them soon. There were only two chairs in the cabin, so she pulled one over to the bed and collapsed into it. Her hands were shaking and, she realized with a start, still covered with blood. She rose and cleaned them in the water, which had cooled to room temperature. Staring at the fire, she realized she would need wood to heat the cabin throughout the night. A few logs stood in a metal bucket nearby and she placed them on the flames, but they would need more.

She went outside in search of the woodpile. She found it to the side of the house. There were sufficient logs, but kindling seemed low. An ax was buried in one of the logs, and Tori assumed they split kindling on an as needed basis. She worked the ax loose. It was surprisingly heavy. She'd never used one before, but how hard could it be? She needed to be careful, however. If she injured herself, both she and Sebastien would certainly die.

She grabbed a log, set it on the ground, lifted the ax above her head and brought it down hard. The blade buried itself in the wood with a satisfying thunk, but the log did not split. Muttering under her breath, she worked the ax free and tried again. This time the log split. She then cut that piece into smaller pieces. She did this with several logs until she thought she had plenty of kindling to keep the fire going. It hadn't been brain surgery, but she'd worked up a sweat and suspected her muscles would ache in the morning. *Oh, for the luxury of central heating.*

She brought the kindling inside, then several larger logs. She placed them in the bucket and went to check on Sebastien. He still appeared to be unconscious, but was mumbling and fidgeting. She placed her hand on his head and his skin burned beneath her fingers. Tori sank into the chair. He had a fever, but she told herself that was normal. The wounds hadn't had time to fester.

Bessie, the slave girl, had told her to keep him hydrated and she knew it to be good advice. She searched the shelves and found a tea canister. She boiled more water and then placed a small amount of leaves inside. As she waited for them to steep, she washed out a few cups. She drank a cup for energy and found it surprisingly good. Then she sat by the bed and tried to spoon the beverage into Sebastien's mouth. Sometimes he swallowed, but sometimes the liquid dribbled out. It was a slow process, but at least she got some fluid into him.

By the time she finished, she was exhausted and starving. She felt bad for eating when Sebastien lay so ill, but needed to keep her strength up. She didn't want to take the time to cook anything, so she ransacked the shelves again, as Bessie had done, and found a jar of fruit. She would go in search of the spring house tomorrow, but it was dark now. She ate the fruit, tossed more wood on the fire and then crawled into the bed and nestled close against Sebastien's fevered body. Roger would come for them. Surely he would come.

Chapter 26

Bob Rivers stared at the blue crystal necklace and ran his index finger along the stone. It didn't feel special, just like any other old rock. But Victoria was not who she claimed to be. Rivers was from the East and knew her eccentricities weren't due to living on the coast. She had told Sebastien that the necklace allowed her to move through time, a notion he found as preposterous as it was beguiling.

"You owe me twenty-five bucks," Dalton said. He seemed nervous and unable to stand still.

Bob, whose real name was Bryce, fingered the broken chain. "How did you get this?"

"Does it matter? One hundred bucks for the necklace—that was the deal."

"You'll be paid," he said trying to smother his feeling of guilt. What did he care if Dalton had killed the girl? Of course, he might need her help to use the thing. He should have thought of that before. "Did you kill her?"

"No, I didn't kill anyone. Not outright. Sebastien's sure to die from his wounds, but he was still alive when I left. I wouldn't have shot him if he hadn't put up a fight."

Bryce waited for a feeling of satisfaction to overcome him at the news of his rival's death, but he felt little more than distaste. He was really bad at the revenge business.

"Don't know if the girl will make it back to the boat. She didn't seem to have much wood sense."

"You left her alone in the woods with a dying man?"

"Just give me my money."

Bryce walked over to his strong box and extracted the agreed-upon sum. "Here. Now go."

"Thought maybe I could work your boat."

Bryce smiled grimly. "Why would I hire someone who just admitted to killing his previous boss?"

"On your orders!" Dalton protested.

"Never say that again if you want to live to see another day. Now go. I don't want to ever see you on my boat again, but I'll hear if you're spreading tales about me."

Dalton shoved the money in his pocket, but left without further protest. Bryce sat at his desk and studied the jewelry. He had joined up with Sebastien, not for mutual protection, but because it made his pilfering from the other man's cargo that much easier. He'd been stealing from Sebastien for a few years now, sneaking on board the *Fury* and lifting a few of the more valuable items. He'd thought to sabotage the other boat on the way down, but the earthquakes had thrown everything into turmoil. Worst of all, however, had been the grudging respect he'd begun to feel for the other man. By the time they had stopped by the Legrand household for Christmas, Bryce had already decided to forgo his revenge. Bankrupting Sebastien might give him some satisfaction, but it wouldn't bring Ari back. Nothing would. It was time he moved on. When he overheard Victoria telling Sebastien that she had come from the future, he knew exactly where he wanted to move on to.

Further examination of the necklace brought no answers. Feeling foolish, he held it in the palm of his hand and tried to will himself into the future. Nothing happened, of course. Perhaps Victoria was merely touched in the head; maybe that was why she acted so strangely and thought she came from a faraway time. Or maybe her story had been yet another lie to hide her true identity from Sebastien.

Frustrated, he shoved the necklace in his pocket. He should never have hired Dalton to do his dirty work. He should have grabbed the girl himself and forced her to tell him how the necklace worked. He couldn't be far behind the *Fury*. He would keep an eye out for the other boat. He might yet have an opportunity to grab the girl.

* * *

When Tori awoke the next morning, the fire had died down and it was cold in the cabin, but the heat Sebastien radiated had kept her warm. She slipped from the bed and added more wood to the fire. Returning to the bed, she stroked Sebastien's dark hair away from his high forehead.

"Sebastien? Can you hear me?" He made no response. Tori swallowed and tried again, forcing a cheerfulness to her voice she didn't feel. "Roger will come for us today. Soon we'll be back aboard the *Fury* and all will be well."

She removed his bandages and saw with relief that the wounds showed no signs of infection. She applied more of the paste, tore fresh strips from her petticoat and re-bandaged him. He stirred when she did this, looking at her through fever-bright eyes and speaking to her in French.

"English, Sebastien," she pleaded. "Remember, I don't speak French."

He blinked. "Victoria."

"Yes." She squeezed his hand, tears coming to her eyes. "You were shot by that crazy old farmer and then Dalton shot you again, but you're going to be all right."

"Dalton... he means to hurt you." His voice trailed off and he muttered something in French.

"Dalton's gone. We're safe." But the moment of lucidity seemed to have passed. Tori made another batch of tea, drinking half and spooning the other half down Sebastien's throat. Then she decided to look for the spring house. She pulled on her coat, hat, and gloves and headed in the direction Bessie had gone yesterday. She kept Sebastien's lessons in mind as she walked, trying to be quiet and observant of her surroundings. Fortunately, there was enough of a trail from the house to the spring that even she could follow it. She soon came upon a small but sturdy structure built like a small log cabin with the roof protruding over the door. She swung the door open and peered into the dim interior. Inside, the walls were roughly plastered. She grabbed a crock of eggs and another of apples. A wheel of cheese and small crock of butter completed her haul. She walked back to the cabin, arms full, but eyes and ears still alert for danger. She saw nothing but trees stripped of their leaves, and the occasional squirrel darting amongst them. There was no sign of Dalton, but she hadn't expected there to be. Having gotten what he wanted, he would have had no reason to stick around.

"I'm going to fix us the best breakfast we've had since leaving New Orleans," she said, although she doubted Sebastien could hear her and knew he would be unable to eat anything. She scoured a frying pan, then fried up a couple of eggs in butter. She ate sitting next to the bed, wondering what she should do. Should she wait for Roger and the other men to find them, or should she go in search of the boat? She wasn't sure she would even be able to find it. The other hunting party should have made their way back yesterday. By then it might have been too dark to send out a search party, but surely they would do so today. Sebastien was their boss. They wouldn't abandon him. Well, not with Roger in charge, anyway. If not for the older man, the others might take advantage of Sebastien's absence to steal the boat and the small amount of cargo it contained.

"Victoria," Sebastien said.

She drew closer to the bed. "Yes, I'm here."

"Don't leave me."

"I won't," she said, wondering how he had known her scattered thoughts. If he wanted her to stay, she would wait for rescue.

Sebastien stilled and appeared to fall into a more restful sleep. Feeling restless, Tori went out to chop more wood, though she hoped they wouldn't need it. When she had a decent pile, she decided to go back to the spring house and clear out what was left of the stores. She could bring them on the *Fury*.

After checking on Sebastien, who seemed less feverish, she set out down the path. There hadn't been a lot of food; the tiny homestead had obviously been struggling for some time. Now she supposed the woods would grow back around it unless someone else claimed the property.

She opened the door of the spring house and stepped inside. There were no more eggs, but a few jars were nestled in the water and there were a few more wheels of cheese. She gathered them up into her skirt and turned to go. As the door swung shut behind her, she caught a glimpse of something out of the corner of her eye. She turned to look, but a blow caught her on the back of the head and everything went dark.

Chapter 27

"Hey, wake up." The words barely penetrated Sebastien's exhaustion. *Why was he so tired? And why did he hurt so badly?* His shoulder burned with pain and his side throbbed in tandem. A hand shook him and he groaned as bolts of agony spread from those two areas. He must have been injured...

"Victoria," he gasped, remembering some of what had happened.

"I've got the men out looking for her," Roger said.

Looking for her? "She was here."

"I'm sure she didn't go far." Roger helped him to a sitting position and waves of pain crashed over him. "What happened here? There's a dead man out front, you look to be in poor shape, and Dalton and Victoria are gone."

Gone? "The old man shot me."

"Thought you were faster than that."

Sebastien ignored the criticism. "Dalton shot the old man and then turned on me. He wanted Victoria."

Roger rocked back on his heels. "Damn, he has Victoria? Who doctored you up?"

"No, he left without her. She took care of me."

"He hurt her? I swear if I ever see that weasel again, I'll shoot him between the eyes."

Sebastien thought back. Everything was a bit foggy, a maze of pain, dizziness, and cold. But he recalled Tori's worried face looking down on him, her mouth swollen. "He hit her."

Roger swore under his breath and Sebastien knew what his friend was thinking. Had Dalton done more than hit her while he was unconscious? "We should have gotten rid of him years ago. Never did like the fellow."

Sebastien agreed, but there wasn't time to worry about past mistakes. "Where is Victoria now?"

"Let me go find out." Roger disappeared from view and Sebastien took a deep breath, regretting the move almost instantly. He was badly hurt, but needed to recover his strength as soon as possible if Victoria was in trouble. Roger finally stepped back in the cabin.

"There's no sign of her. We think we tracked her trail to the spring house. She might have been taken from there."

"Taken?"

"We found this." Roger held up a heavy stick. A smear of blood marred one end and a blond hair was trapped on a twig.

* * *

Consciousness slowly returned, and with it, pain. Tori lay on the hard ground, her battered face pressed against a pile of leaves. When she tried to move, she discovered she was tied at hand and foot.

"About time," a voice said to her left. She recognized the voice, but couldn't match it with a name. "I thought I might have hit you too hard."

"What do you want with me?" she asked, forcing the words past the terror that clogged her throat. She knew the man holding her wasn't Dalton, but who was it? A pair of boots stepped into view and the man knelt beside her.

"I want to know how to work the necklace," Bob Rivers said.

"I don't have it any more. Dalton took it."

"And delivered it to me."

"I don't know how to make it work."

"Not good enough." Rivers grabbed her shoulders and hauled her upright. "You came here from the future. I want to know how."

"I'm telling you the truth—I don't know. That's why I went to the voodoo shop in New Orleans. I thought the shopkeeper might have some answers, but she didn't. She said the power was drained."

"You have a while to think about it. We can't stay here. Sebastien will be after us."

A tear rolled out of her eye. "Sebastien's hurt. You have to take me back to him."

"Not going to happen." He untied her feet. "Get up."

Tori struggled to stand. It was harder than she would have thought without the use of her hands. Her head pounded where Rivers had hit her, and her jaw still hurt from being struck by Dalton. "Just let me go. Do you think I would still be here if I knew how to get home?"

"A good point, but things have been rather crazy since you landed in this century, with the earthquakes and all. You'll have a couple days to think as we make our way north. I suggest you put them to good use."

"Where are we going?"

"Don't you worry about it. I have a destination in mind."

Jerk! He's no different than Ned, Mr. Henderson, or Dalton. "I won't go. Go ahead and shoot me if you want." Brave words. Her stomach rolled as she recalled digging the bullet out of Sebastien's shoulder. Still, she didn't think he would kill her when he thought she had information for him.

"Oh, I think you will. I don't want to hurt you; you already know that. But Sebastien will come after us, if at all possible, and if he reaches us before we reach our destination, I won't hesitate to shoot him."

Tori stared into eyes as hard as ice and didn't doubt he meant what he said. "What is between the two of you? I could tell you disliked one another as far back as Ste. Genevieve." Rivers motioned with the gun and she started walking. They walked in silence for a few moments before he decided to answer her.

"Sebastien took something from me, something dear to my heart. I only want to return the favor."

That didn't make Tori feel any better, for despite the insulting offer he had made her, she knew Sebastien cared for her. He might not love her as she did him, but he cared.

Love? The thought brought her up short, earning her a poke in the back from Rivers' gun. Did she love Sebastien? She loved the way he had made her feel in New Orleans, admired his strength and dependability. When he had fallen lifeless to the ground after Dalton shot him, she'd felt as if her own heart had stopped beating. Did that equal love? She wasn't sure. Love had never factored into her plans. It had been something she'd planned to look for after she was settled, after she had made a mark in her career. Love came with too high a price to give into easily.

They walked all that day, stopping only for brief meals of hardtack and jerky. Tori's legs ached, along with the rest of her. She tried to think about the necklace, about what she could tell him. She remembered the list she had made several weeks ago on the *Fury*. The storm, the river and Mr. Henderson's threats. Let him make of it what he could; it had done her no good.

At last night fell. Rivers made a small fire and tied her feet again. It was cold and even with her coat Tori wondered if she would freeze to death. She knew she wouldn't sleep. She stiffened when Rivers lay down next to her and threw a blanket across both of them.

"Relax, I've no designs on your virtue."

She couldn't relax, at least not at first, trussed up like an animal led to slaughter, fearing for herself and worried about what had happened to Sebastien. Could he really be on their trail? She longed for the safety of his arms, but worried that a hard march across the winter landscape would surely kill him if the bullets hadn't already. She lay stiff and uncomfortable, hating the man at her side and wishing she'd never seen the blue crystal necklace.

Really? A voice whispered in her head. Yes, she would be safe and warm now, snuggled up on Anne's couch, not wondering if today was her last. She would give almost anything to be back there. Everything, perhaps, but the opportunity to be with Sebastien.

Rivers' warmth began to seep into her frozen bones though she wouldn't have thought the man had any warmth to give. Her body ached for rest and she could no longer fight it. She slipped into a light, uneasy sleep.

* * *

"I'll go after her," Roger said. "You can barely stand."

Sebastien continued to dress, bracing himself against the pain as he tugged his boots on. "I have to do this. It's my fault she was taken. If I hadn't brought her on the hunting trip, she'd still be safe on the *Fury*."

"And you would be dead."

"Maybe, maybe not. The old man would still have shot me, but Dalton wouldn't have had a reason to do so."

Roger frowned. "You're in no condition to go. If you think I'm too old, send one of the other men. They aren't all like Dalton. There are a few we can trust."

Sebastien pulled on the fresh shirt Roger had brought from the *Fury*. The one he had been wearing was covered in blood and cut to ribbons. "I have to do this." If he had made Victoria an honorable offer in New Orleans, would this have happened? There was no way to know, but at least things would have been better between them. There was no way he was going to stay behind, but should he send one of the men as well? An uninjured man could travel faster. "It would help if I had a horse. Have you seen any signs of a horse around here?"

"There are a couple of horses in the barn. Not much to look at. Don't think they were being fed regularly and the stalls hadn't been cleaned in days."

"Better than nothing. Saddle up the strongest one for me."

"You'll need food." Roger seemed to have accepted that he wasn't going to talk Sebastien out of going.

"I'll eat something now. Pack whatever else you can find." He wasn't hungry, but knew he had to eat.

Roger brought him a hunk of venison and a piece of hard tack. "The other team shot a deer. By the time they returned to the boat, it was too dark to go in search of your team."

Ignoring the hard tack, Sebastien chewed on the meat. "Which way did they go?"

"North."

"Follow with the *Fury*."

"You know we won't make nearly as good a time as you will on land."

Sebastien nodded. There would be no help from the boat. "Oh, hell, saddle up both horses. I'll bring someone with me."

Roger disappeared and Sebastien forced himself to keep eating. When Roger returned, he said, "I've got Skip saddling the horses. Let's see what they have for supplies." He rummaged through the jars and crocks on the hearth. "Looks like they're nearly cleaned out."

"The place is in bad shape, and I know Victoria used some of the supplies." He could remember the smell of food, although he had found it more nauseating than appetizing at the time.

Roger packed a few things into two saddlebags. "Who's coming with you?"

Sebastien hesitated. His first impulse was to choose Skip or one of the other decent, if rough around the edges, young men on his crew. That way Roger could stay with the *Fury* and keep it out of trouble. But there was too much at stake here. "You're coming. Think Skip can handle command?"

Roger gaped at him. "Me? One of the younger fellows would be faster and handier in a fight. Besides, you've never left the *Fury* in anyone's hands but mine or yours."

"Gotta be a first time. You coming or not?"

Roger drew himself up to his full height, which was a couple of inches above Sebastien's. "Of course I'm coming. I care about the lassie, too."

The two horses, both sorry-looking specimens, stood ready in the yard. Roger slung the saddlebags onto the horses' backs. Sebastien called for Skip. "I'm putting you in charge. Bring the *Fury* as fast as you can upriver, but don't take any foolish risks."

"Me, sir? I've never captained a boat before."

"You can handle it. Put Sparks on the roof. He's got good eyes."

"Be careful, sir, and bring her back. The men all like her fiddling, even if they complain at times."

Sebastien nodded before mounting his horse. By the time he hauled himself into the saddle he was drenched with sweat.

"Gonna make it?" Roger asked under his breath.

"I'll be all right." He turned the horse's head north and Roger followed. They picked up the trail near the spring house. At times the horses slowed them down, for the undergrowth was too heavy for the animals and they had to go around and pick up the trail later, but it was quicker than walking. Victoria and her abductor had a good head start, but would be slowed down by Victoria's inexperience.

They rode for hours. At last Roger called a halt. "It's too dark to see. If we continue on we'll end up laming one of the horses."

Sebastien didn't argue, even though the thought of Victoria at Dalton's mercy—or someone else's—urged him on. He wanted to press forward, but was already swaying with pain and fatigue, barely able to stay on his horse. He could go no farther tonight.

Roger helped him off the horse and settled him against a tree. "Let me take care of the horses and build a fire, then we'll have a bite to eat."

"Sorry I'm not more help."

"Can't believe you made it this far. Rest up—we'll catch them tomorrow. I feel it in my bones."

Sebastien could feel it as well, in his heart as well as his bones. They were close. Almost within reach. But time was running out.

Chapter 28

Darkness still covered the night like a shroud when Sebastien awoke. The remains of a fire glowed to his left and Roger slept within its circle of warmth. Sebastien was still propped against the tree where he had apparently fallen asleep while Roger attended to camp, missing dinner completely. He was hungry now, a sign he was healing. His wounds protested as he pushed himself to his feet, but he moved silently so as not to wake Roger.

He found some dried fruit and hard tack biscuits in with their supplies and nibbled on them, drinking deeply from his water skin. The bone-deep exhaustion from yesterday had eased, but was now aggravated by the itching sense that time was slipping through his fingers.

Roger snored and stirred, but didn't wake. The moon, halfway between full and new, provided a bit of light. Sebastien considered waking Roger, but decided to let the older man sleep. Picking up a stick from the pile of wood Roger had gathered, he scratched a message into the dirt. "Gone ahead."

He saddled his horse, wincing at every clink of the tack, but Roger slept on. The horse balked at leaving the warmth of the fire and heading into the dark, but Sebastien dug his heels into the animal's flanks and it obeyed. Their pace was slow due to lack of light, but with every hour the day brightened and by the time it was full dawn, he had covered a number of miles. Roger would be following him by now, probably cursing him with every breath.

An hour or so after daybreak he found the camp where Victoria and her abductor had slept. He saw the footprints of two people and no sign of blood—encouraging news which tempted him to urge his horse to greater speed.

The animal did its best, but it wasn't long before Sebastien feared he had pushed the horse too hard, for it drew to a halt, dipped its head and moaned. Neither kicks nor slaps to the rump persuaded the horse to move. Instead, it spread its legs as if seeking balance and shuddered. Sebastien patted the horse on the neck and was about to dismount when a roaring sound tore through the air. The trees swayed and the ground rose and fell like waves. This wasn't like the daily aftershocks he'd grown used to; this was another major quake. As Sebastien struggled to stay on the horse's back, a sand boil erupted a dozen feet away, spewing water and black matter into the air. A crevasse opened almost at his horse's feet and a tree snapped and fell into it. His horse neighed and stumbled backward a few feet. Sebastien dismounted and went to the horse's head. Had the animal moved forward as he'd commanded, they might have been on the very ground that had collapsed.

"Good boy," he said, rubbing the horse's face and scratching him behind the ears. The ground continued to roll and it was hard to keep his footing. Water rose in the crevasse and a noxious odor poured forth. From the east he heard the ominous rumbling of banks tumbling into the river, followed by a woman's scream. His head shot up; and without even a thought for his injuries, he leaped across the fissure. His horse whinnied its dismay, but Sebastien didn't look back. He ran toward the river, rising every time the flailing ground through him down. He had to get to Victoria.

* * *

Shortly before dawn, Rivers woke Tori with a nudge of his foot. "We need to get going."

She stirred, realizing she had slept through him untying her feet. She groaned as she tried to rise. Not only did her muscles protest the grueling hike from yesterday, but her feet had fallen asleep and were now assaulted by pins and needles. Rivers moved toward her and she flinched, thinking he was going to strike her. He froze, hand raised, and then slowly reached for her and helped her to her feet.

"I'd untie your hands, but I don't trust you."

Smart thinking. "Don't we get any breakfast? I need my hands to eat."

He considered. "Five minutes." He untied her and gave her another hard tack biscuit and a piece of jerky. Tori ate quickly, knowing he wouldn't give her a minute past the five he had promised. He ate, too, and then offered her a drink of water from his skin.

"Thank you," she said as she passed the skin back to him and then mentally castigated herself as as idiot. Why was she thanking her captor? Was she already falling victim to Stockholm syndrome?

He retied her hands and motioned for her to move out. She did, stepping over logs and other debris. It wasn't easy to keep her balance with her hands tied. "I've thought of all I know about the necklace. I can tell you now and you can let me go."

"Not until we reach our destination."

"Where are we going? I don't think there's any civilization for miles. If Sebastien truly is behind us, you'd better get your information and get out of here."

"Save your breath for walking," he said and gave her a slight shove. Tori stumbled, but regained her footing. The air felt heavy and cold, but the skies appeared clear and she didn't think it was going to snow. She kept moving forward until the monotony of her steps cleared all else from her mind.

"Stop."

Rivers hadn't spoken in hours and the single word, snapped out like a drill sergeant, startled her. She gladly quit moving, taking the opportunity to catch her breath.

"We're out of time. I should have listened to you this morning."

Tori peered into the woods, but didn't see any signs of Sebastien or anyone else coming to her rescue. But if crazy dude was willing to let her go, she wasn't going to argue. "A couple of weeks ago I made a list of everything I could remember before the world turned upside down. I couldn't replicate everything, but I did what I could and nothing happened. The power may be spent."

"I know that's what the voodoo woman told you, but I don't believe it." He pulled the necklace from his pocket. He held it by the chain and the pendant swung between them hypnotically.

"I was arguing with a man. I was upset, scared even. It was snowing, but the sky was filled with thunder and lightning."

Rivers looked skeptical. "Snow *and* a thunderstorm? I've never seen them together."

"Neither had I until that night. It was late, but before midnight. I was near the river. Those are the things I think are important—the river, the time, and the lightning. Maybe my emotions, but I've been upset since then and couldn't get the stone to activate."

"Why do you think it was the stone that brought you here?"

Tori took a deep breath. "The stone got warm against my skin and began to glow." She glanced over at the pendant, which glimmered in the light of the sun, but not with the unworldly glow which had preceded her jump into the past. Even to her own ears the words sounded crazy, and she expected him to erupt in anger. Instead, he grew pensive.

"An energy source. Maybe your voodoo queen wasn't so wrong after all."

Tori shuddered. That mysterious woman wasn't her voodoo queen. "That's all I know. Will you untie me now?"

Rivers didn't seem to hear her. He paced along the shore, talking to himself. "That's it! We haven't had any electrical storms for months. I can't even remember having any last summer." He turned to look at her. "You haven't tried it with lightning again, have you?"

"There haven't been any thunder storms since I came here. Now untie me." Could he be right? Was lightning the missing link?

Rivers tucked the necklace away before approaching her and undoing her bonds. "Is the future as magical as you said?"

"Ordinary people have luxuries that wealthy people in this time couldn't even imagine."

Rivers lifted his head and sniffed at the air like a dog. "You're free to go. Sebastien will come for you. If you both survive." He was acting even stranger than before.

"Survive what?"

"The next earthquake."

Chapter 29

Moments after Rivers' prediction, the quake hit. A thunderous growl preceded the shaking, and then the earth rose and fell in undulating waves, tossing both Tori and Rivers to the ground. Tori stayed where she fell, horrified as the earth mimicked the sea, rippling before her eyes. A lightning bolt struck the ground inches from her face. She recoiled, only to see it happen again, but this time, she realized the lightning came not from the sky, but from the ground itself. She screamed.

"Power!" Rivers yelled. He scrambled to his knees and dug in his pocket for the necklace. To Tori's astonishment, the crystal glowed blue, emitting a pulsing light in the murky fog rising from the ground. Rivers crawled over to her and grabbed her by the arm. "What else do I do?"

Tori pulled off her glove and reached out to touch the stone. She gasped as the heat worked its way into her frozen fingers.

"Victoria!" Rivers shouted in her face, bringing her out of her daze. "What do I do?"

"I don't know. I was scared, I wanted to get away." Her voice shook. She had nearly given up on the chance of returning home. "Think about the future. Picture in your mind."

"How can I do that when I've never been there?" The ground under their feet rose in a sickening wave and then fell, sinking an additional two feet. A rending crack assaulted their ears as a fissure formed in the ground, splitting a grown tree in two like it was a twig. The pendant swayed from side to side on its chain, still admitting the strange light. But had it grown fainter?

"Think of cars and planes. Computers."

"I know nothing of such things." Rivers' grip tightened on her arm. "But you do. You're coming with me."

Why not? It's what she had wanted ever since she had landed in these primitive times—to return to her own world, where she was comfortable. Where a nearly infinite store of knowledge was never more than an arm's length away, where hot and cold water was available on demand, where furnaces and air conditioners kept houses at the perfect temperature. Where she could fly from New Orleans to St. Louis in a matter of hours, rather than months.

Where she had no family and was reduced to sleeping on a friend's couch. A time when Sebastien had already been dead for over a hundred years. She pulled against Rivers' grip.

"Think! There's nothing for me here, hasn't been since Ari died. Take me to your time of wonders."

"Ari?" Had she heard right? The shaking diminished, the roaring abated. "Sebastien's sister? What is she to you?" But Tori didn't really need to ask. She recalled all too well the pain and anger in Sebastien's voice as he talked of his sister's death and the suitor from the East who had abandoned her. "It was you. You're the one who seduced and deserted her." She yanked her arm free.

"I never deserted her. I was coming back; she knew that."

"Sebastien will kill you."

"If he's not already dead."

The words struck her like a physical blow. He had seemed less feverish the last time she had seen him, but he had still been so pale. If Roger and the men had not found him… "He's not dead. And I'm not leaving."

"Victoria!"

She turned at the sound of her name, almost unable to believe her eyes. Sebastien stood at the edge of the woods on the other side of the fissure.

"No! This is my last chance. You're not taking it from me." He snatched Tori and drew her in toward his chest. Out of the corner of her eye she could see the crystal pulse. The air shimmered in its wake.

Sebastien yelled something as he jumped across the cleft, but Tori couldn't hear it. She was back in the apartment with Ned wondering if her self-defense classes had been a waste of time. She slumped in Rivers' grasp, and when his hold loosened, she drove her elbow back as hard as she could. He grunted and released her and she charged forward, toward Sebastien, who was coming equally fast toward her.

They collided in an embrace more painful than romantic. A flash of light came from behind her along with a whooshing sound. Sebastien's arms closed around her.

"I was afraid you would die after Rivers kidnapped me." Tori buried her face into his chest. While she worried that she was hurting him, she needed to feel the solidity of his presence.

"He's gone."

Tori looked up into Sebastien's stunned gaze. Slowly she turned to where, moments before, she had struggled with Rivers. There was no one there. No sign that anyone had ever been there. Rivers and the necklace had vanished. Tori walked to the edge of the river and gazed out, but no, he hadn't jumped or fallen into the water. The water still swirled in an agitated fashion, but unless he had sunk like a stone, he was truly gone. "Do you think he made it? Back to the future?"

Sebastien shook his head as if he still couldn't believe what had happened.

"What if, instead, he went further into the past? What would it be like here in the early 1600s?"

"Few if any whites. Mostly Indians. Serve him right."

Tori shook her head. Even though he had kidnapped her and even knowing what she now knew about him, she didn't wish him dead. "He overheard us on Christmas and sent Dalton to get the necklace."

"That's what Dalton wanted? I thought he wanted you."

"So did I, at first."

Sebastien drew her close. "I'm so glad you're all right."

"Likewise. You were shot. Twice. What are you doing here? You should be back in bed."

"I couldn't lay in bed while you were in danger. Roger came with me. He shouldn't be too far behind. Which reminds me, I had better go see if my horse is still there. When I heard you scream I ran off and left him." He led her along the river and then away from the bank, where they found his horse grazing on what little dormant grass remained.

"He's no beauty, but where did he come from?"

"There were two horses in the barn."

"I never thought to look for horses."

"You had other things to deal with."

That's an understatement. She studied Sebastien. His eyes were bright, but a deep weariness etched his face. She sank to the ground. "Let's wait here for Roger."

After a moment, Sebastien settled in beside her. "Why didn't you go? You've been searching for a way home all this time."

An opportunity that would never come again. The necklace was gone. The enormity of her decision hit her and her hands trembled. She would live the rest of her life in the nineteenth century. With Sebastien, she hoped. "I couldn't leave you." She spoke so softly she wasn't sure he would hear, but nestled against his chest as she was, she felt his heart begin to race.

"I was so afraid you would. Even when I wasn't sure if I believed your wild tale, I worried that you would be taken from me. I'm sorry, Victoria, for what you have given up, but I'm glad the damn thing is gone."

"You're stuck with me now, but I won't be your kept woman, Sebastien. I'll make my own way, somehow."

"No, that was my fault, my mistake. I knew you deserved better, but I let my pride get in my way. Marry me, Victoria. We can buy a house in St. Louis, start a family."

Home and family had always seemed like distant goals in her twenty-first-century life. Something to do once she had established her career. But in truth, she'd never been tempted. None of the men she'd dated compared to Sebastien, with his quiet strength and code of honor. He had his rough edges, of course, but she would smooth them down. "I might take in some pupils."

"Take as many as you like. Just say you'll have me. I'll do the best I can to make it up to you. I don't want you to ever regret this day."

"I'll marry you, Sebastien. Take me to St. Louis." *Take me home.*

Chapter 30

Not long after the quake ended, they met up with Roger. His craggy face brightened when he saw Tori perched in front of Sebastien on the poor malnourished horse.

"Thank God you're all right, lassie. Dalton come back for you?"

Tori shook her head. "It was Bob Rivers. He hired Dalton to steal my necklace, but decided he wanted me as well."

Roger sent Sebastien a long look. "Kill him?"

"No, but I don't think he will bother us again."

"You get her pretty stone back?"

"I'm afraid not, but I'll buy her something to replace it. That necklace has caused a lot of grief anyway."

"Sorry, Victoria. I know you treasured it."

"A good friend gave it to me, but it was time to let it go."

Roger swung off his horse. "Don't think Spindlelegs there will get you both back to the Fury. Tori, take my mount and I will walk."

"Roger—" Sebastien began.

"No arguing. I might be old, but I'm not recovering from two gunshot wounds or a blow to the head."

Sebastien helped Tori slip off his horse and watched as she swung herself in the saddle of Roger's horse. "We will see you back at the boat."

Roger gave him a mock salute and the three began the slow and painful journey back to the *Fury*.

* * *

Sebastien suffered a bit of a relapse after overexerting himself on the rescue mission, but within the week, he was up on the rooftop spotting obstacles, Tori by his side. It would be a bit longer before he could resume poling.

"We'll buy a house once we get to St. Louis. I have some money saved."

"It'll seem strange—but wonderful—to own a house."

"Since it won't have any of your futuristic machines, we will have to hire servants."

Tori made a noncommittal noise. Logically, she knew she was in no way capable of doing everything needed to maintain a home without any of the labor-saving devices she was used to, but still, the thought of having servants seemed very strange to her. "Sebastien, there is something important I've been wanting to talk to you about."

"What?" he asked as he leaned over to brush the hair out of her eyes.

As always, his very touch sent a tingle down her spine. "It's about my friend, Anne, from the twenty-first century."

"I will always be grateful to her that she took you in when you needed help. She was a good friend, no?"

"A very good friend. She works as a tour guide in Ste. Genevieve, and she's the main reason I know as much about this time as I do."

"I know you miss her, but you will make new friends here."

"I'm sure I will, but that's not what I wanted to talk about."

He put his arm around her shoulder. "What then?"

"Your sister... you referred to her as Ari." Rivers had as well, though Tori had yet to tell Sebastien that Rivers was the man who had seduced his sister. The list of people in the twenty-first century that Sebastien wanted to kill was long enough already. "Was that short for Arianne?"

"I don't wish to discuss my sister. What happened to her is in the past. Please leave it there."

"That's just it. I'm not sure that's true. Anne gave me the necklace, Sebastien. I met her four years ago when she was a patient of my mother's at the hospital. She was admitted with life-threatening complications due to labor, but the advanced medicine of my time was able to save her and the baby."

She could feel the tension in Sebastien's body and sensed that he knew where she was going with this—knew, and both feared and longed for it to be true. "Even with modern medicine, it was a near thing, and she and the baby spent time in the hospital. She said she couldn't remember how she had come to be by the side of the road, near the river. Some people driving by spotted her and called for help. As far as I know, she never recovered her memory. She is a single mother raising her daughter on her own. She goes by the name Anne Rush."

He sucked in a breath of air. "You think Anne Rush could be my sister? That Ari is alive and well, although beyond our means to contact her?"

"I think it's possible."

Sebastien was quiet for so long she didn't think he was going to speak. "Describe your friend to me," he said at last.

"She has long dark hair and brown eyes. She's slim with a rather athletic build."

"I don't know. That describes Ari, but also thousands of other young women."

"If I could draw, I would sketch her, but I'm horrible at drawing."

"Just in case, tell me something about the little girl."

"I'm not that good with kids."

He chuckled. "So you paid her little heed?"

"She has dark hair and eyes like her mother. She likes spaghetti." Tori remembered that last night, when she had made dinner and the toddler had gotten it all over her face.

"I don't know what spaghetti is."

"Long narrow noodles in tomato sauce."

"Doesn't sound very appetizing."

"Trust me, it's delicious. Hannah seems like a typical kid. Plays with toys, loves her mom."

"Hannah." He tried the name out on his tongue. "I would like to think that Hannah is my niece and Ari is well."

Tori heard the uncertainty in his voice. "I know, it's a lot to take in." She had begun to put the clues together when Rivers raved had about his Ari as he held the blue crystal necklace Anne had given her. In the days since, she had come to believe that her theory was correct, but there was no way to prove it. It might take a while for Sebastien to accept, although she hoped he would eventually find comfort in it.

As for her, she had found her place on the river along with her riverman. She would miss the luxuries of the future, but no longer desired to trade her current life for her former life—in the future. *It's all so confusing.* She was glad that Rivers was gone, glad that he had taken the necklace with him. She had all that she needed in the here and now.

Epilogue

Bryce sat up, his head pounding and nausea churning in his stomach. What was he doing lying on the ground? It was cold, but he was dressed warmly and didn't seem to be injured. As he tried to recall what he'd been doing prior to passing out, he remembered the earthquake.

Of course! He'd felt the tingling in his legs that signaled another massive shaking. Something may have fallen on him, or perhaps he'd hit his head upon falling to the ground. That would explain both his headache and the fact that he appeared to be napping in the middle of nowhere in the middle of the day.

He had been with someone. Victoria. Yes, it was all becoming clear. He had kidnapped Victoria so she could tell him how to work the time travel device. Turned out she hadn't known much. At first he had assumed she was lying to him, but by the time the quake struck and Sebastien arrived, he was fairly certain she had shared all she knew—and guessed—about the object's power.

He glanced around the clearing. No sign of either Sebastien or Victoria. They must have escaped while he was unconscious. He was damn lucky they hadn't killed him. Victoria must not have told Sebastien who he truly was, or he had no doubt the riverman would have taken his revenge on the man who had seduced his sister.

He scrambled to his feet, surprised that the earth was so still. After the first two major quakes, aftershocks had torn the earth apart for days. In truth, there had not been a single shake-free day since December sixteenth, though the intensity of the aftershocks had diminished the farther they traveled from New Madrid. It felt unnatural for the earth to be so still.

He remembered a large fissure opening in the ground not far from where he stood, but it must have closed, for he saw no evidence it had ever existed. He shuddered, glad he hadn't been inside the crevasse when the earth slid it closed.

He took stock of his situation. His pack of supplies still clung to his back, so he had food, water and his bedroll, but he needed to head back to the *Revenge*. Once he was safely on board, he would decide what to next. It seemed unwise to return to St. Louis, but he could take the keelboat up the Ohio and sell it. He was done with the boating business, although after seeing the glory of the New Orleans, he might invest some money in steamboats. As he struck out in a southern direction, a hint of blue caught his eye. He bent, picking up the necklace that had caused him so much trouble. Victoria treasured it, so he was surprised they had left it behind. Guessing it might have some value, he stuffed it in his pocket. He berated himself for having fallen for the story she'd told Sebastien at Christmas. Time travel, indeed. He'd had a lot to drink that night, but even in the cold light of day he hadn't realized how ridiculous her tale was. When he thought about how he had prepared for this day, he almost wanted to laugh at himself, but by burying a considerable chunk of his fortune prior to hiring that fool Dalton to steal the necklace, he'd done nothing but throw obstacles in his own way. Now he would have to go dig up his money before selling the *Revenge* and returning to the East Coast.

The air was heavy and still. He heard no birds chattering or small animals scampering through the underbrush. Wildlife acted strangely around the earthquakes and had probably not yet recovered. Bryce made his way to the river, noting that the foliage seemed less thick than he remembered. When he gazed down at the flat, brown expanse of the mighty river he gasped and nearly lost his balance. Where was the Mississippi he knew? Where was that wild, curling beast choked with trees and branches, spinning in whirlpools and dangerous currents? The river he saw before him had been dredged of its hazards and looked placid and calm, although he knew that could be an illusion. He saw no keelboats or flatboats, although in the distance he saw a large, low-lying vessel. The time traveling device had worked. He was no longer in his own time, although he couldn't be certain he had traveled to Victoria's time. The earthquake could not be responsible for the depth of change he saw here, only the long march of time.

Bryce drew a deep breath of air into his lungs. It wasn't as sharp or pure as what he was used to, but neither was it the noxious fumes loosed by the earthquakes. He wished he had spent more time questioning Victoria about the future, but he'd been focused on learning how to work the necklace. He couldn't believe he had actually succeeded.

With a new spring in his step, he changed directions, heading up river to where he had buried his money. He was on the west bank and had buried his funds on the east bank, but surely he could find a way across. Until then, he had his store of food and a few coins in his pocket, although he wasn't sure they would still be good. He had his gun, so he could always hunt, though the curious lack of animals continued.

After he walked a few miles, he heard a noise he couldn't place. It was loud and came and went with some degree of regularity. The volume increased the farther he walked and when he stumbled upon the strangest road he had ever seen, he knew it was the source of the racket. The road wasn't dirt or wood or cobbled stones, but a wide expanse of some hard rock-like material. As he stood there, wondering whether or not he should follow the road, the sound came again and a box like object hurtled down the road at astonishing speed. A horn sounded and Bryce stepped back onto the grass just as the object flew by, sending a cloud of dust his direction.

His heart hammered as he walked alongside the road, careful not to step on the hard surface again. Another object, similar to the first, blew past him. This must be the way people traveled in this time, although he could not imagine what they used to propel the carriages. They weren't pulled by horses, and horses would have never been able to run that fast. He heard another sound, this one over his head, and looked into the sky to see a dart-shaped object, definitely not a bird, flying overhead. He stumbled. Were people inside that thing as well? Could people in this time fly like birds?

Bryce acknowledged to himself that he had not prepared as adequately for this challenge as he had thought. He had wanted to glimpse the wonders Victoria had described, but had not expected the world to be so radically changed. Still, he thought himself up for the challenge. He had never been one to back away from a fight. He was more excited than anxious as he continued on his way, the miles melting under his ground-eating stride. He had much to learn and experience, and it was only when he thought of the river, flowing deep and dark and deceptively calm that his breath caught in his throat. He'd thought the Mississippi something that could never be conquered, but here it was, altered beyond recognition. He would do well to recall that adventure never came without danger. Nothing he couldn't handle, however. He squared his shoulders and walked alongside the road as the sun climbed higher in the sky. A new world awaited him.

Cathy Peper

Cathy Peper lives in the Midwest with her husband, three children and a very spoiled mid-sized dog named Tiny. A lifelong reader, she is now enjoying her lifelong dream of being an author and bringing the types of stories she loves to read to other readers. In the rare moments when it's not too hot, too cold or raining, you might find her bicycling to the winery to kick back, relax and drink wine.

In addition to time travel romances, Cathy enjoys writing historical and paranormal romances as well as mystery and suspense novels.

Sign up for my newsletter at:
http://eepurl.com/bBiwvj and receive a **Free** Regency short story as well as news about upcoming releases.

Connect with me:
Email: clpeper@charter.net
Website: cathypeper.com
Facebook:
https://www.facebook.com/cathy.peper.9http://eepurl.com/bBiwvj

Made in the USA
Coppell, TX
16 December 2019